**Richard had never been one to believe in love at first sight. But, maybe, love in the first twenty-four hours?**

It sounded so sappy. Love was a relationship that developed over time when two people had the same likes and dislikes, or the same goals for the future.

But now, tonight, sitting here in the flickering firelight, Richard thought that attraction, the need to hold and care for Samantha despite the fact that they were from two different worlds, and that feeling inside him, the one that said this was the woman for him, was more important than anything else.

**Books by Cheryl Wolverton**

Love Inspired

*A Matter of Trust* #11
*A Father's Love* #20
*This Side of Paradise* #38
*The Best Christmas Ever* #47
*A Mother's Love* #63
*\*For Love of Zach* #76
*\*For Love of Hawk* #87
*What the Doctor Ordered* #99
*\*For Love of Mitch* #105
*\*Healing Hearts* #118
*\*A Husband To Hold* #136
*In Search of a Hero* #166
*†A Wife for Ben* #192
*†Shelter from the Storm* #198
*\*Once Upon a Chocolate Kiss* #229

\*Hill Creek, Texas
†Everyday Heroes

## *CHERYL WOLVERTON*

RITA® Award finalist Cheryl Wolverton has well over a dozen books to her name. Her very popular HILL CREEK, TEXAS series has been a finalist in many contests. Having grown up in Oklahoma, lived in Kentucky, Texas and now Louisiana, Cheryl and her husband of twenty years and their two children, Jeremiah and Christina, consider themselves Oklahomans who have been transplanted to grow and flourish in the South. Readers are always welcome to contact her via: P.O. Box 106 Faxon, OK 73540, or e-mail her at Cheryl@cherylwolverton.com. You can also visit her Web site at www.cherylwolverton.com.

# ONCE UPON A CHOCOLATE KISS

## CHERYL WOLVERTON

*Love Inspired.*

Published by Steeple Hill Books

STEEPLE HILL BOOKS

Steeple
Hill®

ISBN 0-373-87236-4

ONCE UPON A CHOCOLATE KISS

Copyright © 2003 by Cheryl Wolverton

Visit us at www.steeplehill.com

**Printed in U.S.A.**

Truthful lips endure forever,
but a lying tongue lasts only a moment.
—*Proverbs* 12:19

Patience Smith, to whom I submitted this years ago.
She loved it, and because of her encouragement,
I never forgot this story.

Lori Linxwiler, who willingly gave me information
I needed from a nurse's point of view.
Let's face it, it's been twenty years
since I've been a paramedic! Thanks, Lori!

The fans who demanded more
HILL CREEK, TEXAS stories.

And my family, who, when this story
absolutely flooded my being, didn't make me stop,
but allowed me to write to my heart's delight.

# *Chapter One*

*December 31, Hill Creek, Texas*

"Oh! I'm sorry!"

Thirty-six-year-old Richard Reilly Moore caught the young woman who had just collided into him outside the church doors, hardly registering her apology. He danced on the icy steps and held on to the shifting, slipping woman for dear life, trying to keep both her and himself from tumbling down the steps.

"Yikes. Wai-ai-ai-ait! O-o-o-oh!" The woman's voice squeaked with each word. Richard sucked in a sharp breath. "Whoa! Just hold still!"

It was to no avail. He lost his footing. So did the woman. Tangling together was inevitable. They went down.

The only thing Richard could do was wrap his arms around the woman and pray God would protect them both. Holding her closely, he bounced, slid and rolled until, with a loud *thud,* they hit the snow piled up along the sidewalk. Pain ricocheted through his feet, back and elbows. No one had heard or seen them land in an ignominious heap. Most of the residents were in church already. He had been running late.

She had simply been running.

He ignored the elbow in his ribs and cracked open an eye to see what other surprises the bundle of energy had in store for him. He couldn't believe what he saw, so he popped open the other eye to make sure. His vision hadn't disappointed him.

Laying atop of him and looking rather shocked was a beautiful petite blonde who was quite flustered and out of breath. But she wasn't just beautiful—for Richard had seen some of the most stunning women in the world—she was more. Her blue eyes sparkled with the emotions she felt— and they were certainly running the gamut as she stared down at him in surprise, recognition of their predicament and then dawning embarrassment.

"I don't suppose this is the time to crack a blonde joke," he asked dryly, unable to resist responding to the rising color in her cheeks.

Blue eyes twinkled with sheepish humor. "Only if I can crack a British joke. Or Scottish or—"

"Close enough," he replied, surprised she'd heard the slight Irish brogue in his speech that sometimes came out more British than Irish. He'd attended an English boarding school. His thoughts quickly changed from curiosity to pain when the woman scrambled to get off him. How could someone so alive and vibrant yet so tiny manage to elbow or knee every sore spot on his body?

"Here, let me help you." She grabbed his arm, insistent on aiding him.

"Really, I think I'm fine. Just snow-covered," he replied. The last thing he wanted was to risk allowing this woman to pull him up and accidentally knock him right back over. He managed to get to his feet before he found out he was quite wrong about being fine. His eyes widened with pain as he tried to put weight on his left foot.

"You're hurt!"

A dull flush entered his cheeks. The pride in him wanted to deny he had hurt his ankle in that fall. But the inability to walk kept him from telling a falsehood. Trying to be gallant about the entire thing he replied, "At least you made it out in one piece. Care to tell me what had you rushing from church?"

"I wasn't rushing from church," she argued, moving forward to brush the snow from him.

He couldn't help but notice how small her hands were as they brushed over his shoulders, down his arms and chest. Catching at her hands, he murmured, "I'm fine—if I can find somewhere to sit down."

"Oh!"

She avoided his grasp like an eel slipping from a fisherman's hands and anchored an arm around him. The tiny arm was really quite ridiculous around his six-foot tall frame. But the woman was insistent on helping him.

"Lean on me," she commanded.

For one so small, she was quite authoritative. He grinned in amusement and gave her a bit of his weight. His grin quickly turned to a grimace when he tried to put weight on his foot.

Why had this happened now? He didn't have the time. He had so many other things to do. The woman urging him forward drew his mind from thoughts of work. Glancing down, he realized she really was putting her all into helping him over to a safe place to sit.

"I wasn't—" *huff, huff,* he heard as she danced around in her need to assist "—leaving. I had forgotten my purse and was going back to get—" *huff* "—it."

As she moved back and forth, weaving around the piles of snow, he again noted how her head barely came to his eye level. She certainly was cute—especially in this nurturing mode. She didn't even know who he was and yet she was trying to help him. How odd. People only helped someone like him to get what they could, but this woman—his ankle was really beginning to hurt— this woman didn't have any idea who he was. Distracted by the pain, he let her assist him to sit on the edge of the circular fountain that was turned off for winter. He reached down to slip his shoe and sock off to examine the swelling.

"Oh dear. That's very purple."

Glancing up, he noted the worry on the young

woman's face. She looked genuinely contrite. "I'll be fine," he said, trying to reassure her.

"I wonder if it's broken."

Moving it carefully around, he finally shook his head. "I don't think so. But I do believe it is quite bummed up."

The woman bounced back and forth in front of him, wringing her hands. Richard watched her, wanting to reach out and grab her to calm her down. She really was concerned.

When was the last time anyone had worried about him? He shook his head. Reaching out, he gave in to impulse and caught her hand. The chill in her fingers filtered through his leather gloves. Frowning, he pulled her down next to him. "You shouldn't be out like this," he murmured, and took her hands between his own to warm them.

"I'll be fine. It's you I'm worried about."

She had a valid point. His ankle was really hurting now. "I'll be fine...I think." Glancing around, he noted there wasn't a cab in sight. "You can make it up to me by calling a cab for me so I can get back to my hotel," he suggested, hoping to pacify her. His friend Dillon was certainly going to get a laugh out of this. Richard had arrived only last night and wasn't due in for another few days at the store, though he'd stopped in really late to check things out. Dillon had wanted to talk to him, spend some time with him, and Richard had agreed. At loose ends, he'd decided to attend the midnight church service to welcome in the New Year. He'd promised himself to get back into church—at least while no one knew who he was, he thought wryly. Here, he didn't have to hide out. Especially since most people wouldn't associate him with the world-famous confectionery shop Dunnington's, since the business had been in his mother's family until just ten years ago, when Richard's father was named CEO. In the business world everyone knew who he was. But here, people didn't. It was so very refreshing.

"A cab? *Hotel?* Oh dear. You're new here!" She stilled for the first time since she'd run him over, and studied him.

The odd look she gave him as her gaze ran over his face, his nose and his eyes made him wonder if she suddenly had recognized him. He wasn't sure if her gaze was a good thing or not.

"Tell me tonight wasn't your first time at church here," she continued.

Slowly, with a grin, he nodded. "I'm afraid so. I just got into town last night."

She groaned and dropped her chin against her chest. "I am really sorry. Oh dear, I can't believe this!" She sounded very distressed. She nibbled her lip before glancing first to her left and then to her right, as if looking for help from some passerby or maybe even a cab to shove him into so she could relieve her embarrassment.

"Tell you what, let me take you to the local hospital and see that your foot is fixed up—"

"No hospital." He immediately vetoed that. If he ended up in a hospital, Dillon would never let him live it down. "I've had worse injuries before, Miss…?

"Sam. Sam Hampton."

"Sam…?"

The surprise in his voice earned him a chuckle. "Actually, it's Samantha but everyone calls me Sam."

"And I'm Richard Moore. Nice to meet you." When he saw no reaction to his name, his smile widened. Having this woman care for him and be concerned for him without knowing he was one of the Dunningtons really threw him for a loop.

It felt good—and so different from all the phoniness in the world he lived in.

"Now, there's a lie!" she said chuckling.

At first he thought she'd discerned his identity, but then he realized her mind was on something totally different. She was still embarrassed over having leveled him flat like a linebacker for the Dallas Cowboys. Lifting a brow, he said gently, "What? You think I lie when I say I'm pleased to meet you?" His gaze traveled over her and he realized just how nice it had been to meet this woman. "I wouldn't be so sure of that."

This woman had certainly caught his attention from the start. Richard had always been too busy, too caught up in work to have time for life. Until a moment ago.

"Well," Samantha said, her cheeks turning pink, "if you won't let me take you to the hospital then at least let me take you to my home and put some ice on that ankle."

"Are you sure it won't be any trouble?" he asked, surprised at her openness. Most women wouldn't offer such a thing. He'd never met a woman that innocent and willing to help—unless she had ulterior motives.

Richard knew well that people usually weren't

what they seemed. Maybe that was why this woman was so refreshing. She wasn't like the go-getters and manipulators he'd dealt with in the past. She was open and honest. The barely contained energy this woman had, as she rushed about and spoke what was really on her mind, not some veiled agenda, intrigued him.

"None at all. It's the least I can do. Let me go get my car."

Before he could protest, the small—and fast—woman was up and hurrying across the parking lot.

He wondered if he should call a cab. He was a Christian—had been raised in church and given his life to God at an early age. True, he'd been busy lately and hadn't spent as much time as he should with God—sometimes life seemed to get in his way. But this evening it hadn't. This evening, for the first time, he'd met someone who was a breath of fresh air. He wouldn't want to compromise her by going to her house. Small-town gossip could be cruel.

Shaking his head, he thought again how unique it was for someone to be as concerned about him as this woman was. He thought about her offer. What would it hurt to go home with her, let her treat his foot and spend a few hours just chatting? The woman was harmless enough. He grinned at that thought.

His foot certainly didn't agree with him.

And it was nice that she didn't know who he was. No bowing and scraping from her, or worse, freezing up and refusing to talk to him because he was rich. He just didn't want that again, he thought wearily.

As he waited, he pulled his coat closer against the cold air that blew through the sleeping oak trees that dotted the church's landscaped grounds. Asleep for the winter, they had no leaves or greenery. Instead, their brown branches were coated with a layer of fine white snow. As the wind blew, those branches smashed together, sending a thin misting of snow over everything.

A few had icicles hanging from them, just as the building did. Lights dotted the huge lawn, shining in different directions, several lighting up the manger scene that sat on the corner of the lot.

The rest of the lights allowed shadows to be cast. He could hear music inside, as the service was already under way.

He heard the approaching noise of a vehicle traveling over the snow- and sand-covered street.

As the engine's hum grew louder, it pulled Richard's attention toward the street.

The woman drove up to the curb in a tiny red pickup truck that had seen better days. She waved at him, her engaging smile shining across the short distance. Any thoughts he'd had about the past pain and disillusionment of life and people fled at the sight of that sweet, gentle expression that graced her face. He stood, transfixed by that smile. Unfortunately, reality intruded in the form of pain, and, to his utter embarrassment, he had to hop as best he could toward the truck.

Chuckling, the woman came forward. "I hate to say this, but have you ever played hopscotch?"

Grinning, he shook his head.

"Well," she said, pulling open the creaking rusty door, "sometimes the players are wonderful at it, other times they wobble around, right?" Her eyes twinkling, she continued, "You look like the wobbling ones at the moment."

He chuckled. "I do, do I?"

She grinned cheekily. "By the way, I live two blocks away. Normally I don't bring my truck, but I had to make a pickup on the way and so I drove. Oh," she added, giving him a very stern warning glance. "I don't normally pick up strangers either. I'm not alone where I'm going."

"An injured man doesn't have much room to argue, madam, what form of transportation he takes. And rest assured, you will be safe with me."

Glancing worriedly at his foot she nibbled her lip again. "We'll get you right over to my house and get something on that."

If she was relieved at his words, he didn't see it in her expression. Her attention had returned strictly to the injury.

Helping him into the vehicle, she waited until he was snug with his seat belt fastened before closing the door.

He adjusted the tan belted coat and then, in as dignified a manner as possible, folded his black nylon sock and slipped it into the empty charcoal loafer in his lap.

Samantha jumped into the truck, pausing to tuck the bottom of her blue dress well in from the closing door. She adjusted the beat-up gray jacket she wore over it and then fastened her seat belt. In moments she made a U-turn in the middle of the vacant street and took off the way she'd come. The tiny vehicle was toasty warm, the vents chugging out an air current strong enough to ruffle his hair. He felt his cheeks thaw and begin to heat.

A trash bag hung over the standard stick shift,

and between the driver and passenger windshield was a sticker of a cartoon character. Stickers and trash cans. Two things not in his expensive car or any car he'd driven in for quite a while.

"It's quiet this time of the evening," he murmured over the engine's noise.

"Everyone is in church. Hill Creek, Texas, may only run twenty thousand or so, including the outlying areas, but most everyone attends church."

They did pass a few cars, belying Samantha's claim. He wondered if she exaggerated everything, and decided that must be part of her outgoing personality. She hadn't exaggerated where she lived, though, he realized when she turned two blocks later.

As he watched her drive down the street, he opened his mouth to mention the new building two blocks down where the street dead-ended into Hill Creek's new mall, which this farming community certainly was proud of. Dunnington's was very visible; the main store was surrounded by large gray sections of wall that blocked the current entrance while engineers and such worked on the inside of the store.

She had an excellent view of what was going on at the construction site, he realized. Hoping to gauge her reaction to the mention of his business, maybe find out just what she thought about someone like him in general, he opened his mouth to ask her about Dunnington's.

The woman beat him to that. ''Over here is where I live and over there is the devil's playground.''

Blinking, Richard stared at where she pointed and then looked back to her. Though she pointed at the construction site down at the mall, she had to be talking about the hardware store or perhaps something he hadn't seen. Words like that from such a sweet young woman were so out of character.

''Devil's playground?'' he asked, certain the astonishment could be heard in his voice. He was lucky that he could get that out through his windpipe. It'd nearly closed at her words. She pointed at the mall again.

He simply shook his head, certain he'd missed something.

''Yeah. Well, that's what some of us have taken to calling it. It's rather bad of me, I know. But they're bringing in a store that is going to be my competition.''

Then he saw what she meant. ''You own a candy store?'' he asked, taking in the tiny gin-

gerbread-like building that advertised homemade
confections as well as "lunch items."

She turned in beside the shop and then slipped
the brake on before she opened her door. She slid
out and came around to the other side of the vehicle. "Yeah. I sure do. And that new company
that faces this way from the mall?" She gestured
down the street. "It's here to put me out of business."

Before he could reply, Samantha slipped her
arm around him and led him toward the side door
of the building. Unlocking it, she guided him inside.

Dark it might be, but he recognized well the
smell of a confectioner's shop. How could he not?
He'd been raised in one himself.

But unfortunately, he was afraid that when this
woman, this angel of mercy and simple beauty
found out who he was, she was going to break
his other foot before booting him right out the
front door. How could he go about telling her that
her conqueror and savior was the devil that was
going to put her out of business?

# *Chapter Two*

"I really don't want to put you out."

Samantha smiled at the man. How could she not? He was gorgeous. He was polite. He was gentle. She could go on and on with the impression he'd made on her, but didn't.

"You aren't putting me out at all."

She wondered what the man thought of her candy shop. She paused here at the front end of the store where they had entered. A tiny light on the counter illuminated the front of the shop at night, allowing Mr. Moore to see around him.

She tried to see The Candy Shoppe through a stranger's eyes. A black and white picture of her grandparents, from the newspaper, when they opened the shop aeons ago, hung on the wall to her right. Various articles surrounded it. The announcement about adding lunchtime meals was beside those, a testament to her needing to add more to keep the store open and draw in more people.

On the other wall were professional pictures of candy and flowers hanging in a gilded frame. Wainscoting climbed halfway up the wall. Above it was a soft pastel wallpaper of blue, pink, yellow and green. Old-fashioned wrought-iron tables, in various pastel shades, dotted the sturdy wood floor. Of course, behind the counter the floor became cement.

Oh, the memories. Some of her best times had been in this shop with her grandmother—getting to help mix the candy, playing ballerina while Granny cleaned up at night.

Memories to fill the places that should have been made with parents who were absent most of her childhood. Especially her father.

"Nice," the man murmured.

Jolted into action by the deep soft voice, Samantha moved to the end of the counter and lifted part of the Formica-covered countertop.

Richard hobbled through it.

Samantha waited until he was through before slipping her arm back around him.

He fit her perfectly, she thought, as she tried to help him limp through the public area and into the back communal living room.

''What happened!'' Angela McCade, sitting on the sofa, book in her lap, jumped up from her seat.

''Meet Angela, one of my boarders,'' Samantha said. ''This is Richard Moore,'' Samantha said to Angela, who came forward to help.

''Nice to meet you,'' Richard said, and Samantha thought again what a wonderful voice he had.

She helped him get seated on her sofa. ''Well,'' she breathed out, tired from trying to help the huge man. ''Welcome to my home.'' It was nearly a question.

Richard put her instantly at ease. ''It's beautiful.''

Samantha felt herself blushing. He looked right at home in her living room, she thought. She couldn't believe her reaction to him. He was too handsome and too charming.

She was in so much trouble.

She had better keep her mind on other things.

''What happened to your ankle?'' Angela asked.

"I'll be right back," Samantha murmured to Mr. Moore, sitting on the overstuffed sofa, his shoe and sock lying next to him. "Angie, why don't you help me?"

She turned and headed toward the back room, past the old elevator that led up to her grandmother's extra rooms, where Samantha had lived for several years. She crossed the cement floor to the freezer located in a small storeroom near the back door. Angela was right on her heels, her long golden-brown hair flopping in a ponytail.

When they were out of earshot, Angela asked, "Where'd you get the knight in shining armor?" Her light blue eyes flashed with curiosity as she waited for Samantha to explain.

Samantha shook her head at her young friend. "I didn't 'get' him anywhere. And though I will agree he certainly has knight qualities—" like being the most gorgeous man she'd ever met…she allowed her smile to fade "—I'm afraid he didn't rescue me. Exactly."

At the last word Angela groaned. "What did you do this time?"

"Hey, it's not always my fault," Samantha protested, hunting through the dim supply room's shelves until she found the ice pack. Going to the huge steel freezer, she pulled it open and patiently filled the bag. Unfortunately, Angela knew her too well. When Angela simply stood there, her arms crossed, Samantha sighed. "Okay. Okay. I had forgotten my purse in the truck and was in a hurry to get it because I hadn't locked the doors."

"*You* did that to his foot?" Angela exclaimed. Angela had many sounds, good and bad. This one was definitely chastising in its own way, with a hint of *I knew it* added in for good measure.

Samantha simply nodded. At only twenty-two Angela had the ability to make the older Samantha feel like a little kid. "It was an accident."

"You were worried about today, weren't you?" Angela asked, referring to a meeting they'd had earlier to discuss the store's condition.

Samantha sighed. "Maybe a bit distracted."

Angela reached out and touched Samantha's arm. "Don't be. The business hasn't failed yet. We still have Valentine's Day to pull it out of the red."

"But we didn't at Christmastime," she said quietly.

They'd been through so much together in the past five years. Angela had come to work for her when she was seventeen and had worked her way through college in this shop while pursuing her veterinarian degree. She was Sam's assistant manager and definitely someone she confided in.

Since her grandmother's first major stroke fifteen years ago, Samantha had been struggling to make a success of this store. Her mother hadn't wanted anything to do with it—until her grandmother became an invalid. And then she only wanted it for the money she could milk out of it for her drinking habit. That had ended five years ago when her mother ran off with some trucker passing through town. Her mother died a month later in an accident. Unlike her mother, Samantha loved the store. She could remember the excitement of standing on a footstool so she could reach the cabinets to help stir the fudge, learning how to tell by smell and feel if the confections were just right. Fifteen years she'd worked to keep the store running. Everyone in the area knew and loved the candy she made. But new people were moving in, new stores, new competition that had the money to put into advertising and mass marketing of their goods. New malls were opening, like the one out on the edge of town. A tricounty area endeavor, this mall was going to revive all of the nearby towns and give people a place to go other than the bigger cities, which were located as close as a couple of hours from here.

"Maybe our Christmas sales weren't the best, but I bet that store down the street isn't going to be open by Valentine's Day. They still have too much work to do. So that means we still have a chance to turn this place around."

"You've been talking to my father," Samantha said curtly. Her father wasn't around much, but whenever he had a job in town, he made sure to stop by, or to pump Angela for information. And Angela always imparted the information that Samantha's father passed on to her.

Angela shrugged. "I was at the Mexican restaurant and he happened to be there too, and I asked him about Dunnington's."

Her father had worked on many projects at the mall since it'd gone up this year. Samantha didn't need her father's ill-timed advice when she was struggling for her very livelihood.

"I'm only concerned about the store," Angela said softly to her boss.

Lately Samantha simply wanted to give up and say God had forsaken her. Why had she struggled so hard with this store, only to see it sinking now? Putting her father to the back of her mind, she concentrated instead on what Angela had said about Valentine's Day.

"I don't know, Angie. I'm not sure I even have enough money to keep us afloat until February. I do know it's going to take a miracle to keep this place open, though."

"It's all Dunnington's fault," Angela said now.

Ten years ago Dunnington's Incorporated had decided to leave the shores of Ireland and the surrounding area and travel West. Landing in America like the pilgrims of so long ago, Dunnington's had forged ahead to explore the new country and stake its claim. In a short time it had opened its first overseas store in New York City, and the previously unknown company had been an instant success. The ability to walk in and get whatever one wanted from whatever part of the world one wanted had intrigued the public as much as the way Dunnington's advertised its store.

"They certainly haven't helped, especially with their ad campaign," Samantha admitted, thinking about how smart they'd been with their commercials, and how much money and time they devoted to advertising.

The commercial she most remembered was their first one, which had actually been one of the original commercials from Ireland. It opened with a young man dressed in a kilt, walking out, bagpipes in hand. He ambled across a grassy knoll with a loch in the background. A soft wind blew, whipping at the edge of his red, yellow and green kilt, causing the white shirt to ripple across his body as he walked. And he played a beautiful old love song—''Greensleeves.'' Then others appeared in the background, in the slight fog that blew as they walked, and the young man let go of the pipe and began to sing in a gentle Irish brogue.

Dunnington's had been smart, all right. Its commercial could sell anything.

''Still, you have to admit, though they had a great campaign, they didn't have any stores here,'' Samantha added. ''So, that isn't the root of our problems.''

Finally, Angela spoke. ''I guess you don't want Uncle Mitch to run them out of town?'' she quipped.

Samantha laughed, though it was tinged with a bit of melancholy. ''I don't think that falls within the sheriff's job, Angie,'' she said wryly.

Angela shrugged. ''Well, God can work bigger

miracles than the luck of that Irishman can boast stores.''

Samantha nodded. ''Anyway,'' she said, dragging her friend back to the present, ''I don't want to rehash anything more about that nightmare down the street and how it's going to affect our business.''

She took a deep calming breath.

''Here.'' She shoved the ice pack at Angela. ''Go put this on our guest's foot while I make him up some hot chocolate. How's Granny?'' she asked as she closed the freezer and turned toward the kitchen. Angela blocked her way.

''Granny's fine. She's finally asleep. But I want to hear the rest of this before I go,'' she protested, not moving aside to allow Samantha to pass.

At least she wasn't rehashing their financial state, Samantha thought. So, she answered quickly, hoping to put it to rest. ''I ran the man over. I hurt him and offered him a place to get some treatment since he wouldn't go to the hospital and is new to town.''

''You ran him over? In the truck?''

Samantha frowned. ''No, I ran into him and knocked him down.''

''He's new to town?'' Angela asked.

Samantha sighed. "Yes. He's new here. Got in last night," Samantha finally said, staring at Angela and waiting.

"You certainly learned a lot about him in a short time," Angela said, lifting her eyebrows.

*Uh-oh,* Samantha thought. "I did not," she protested. "I just, um…" She shrugged, unable to come up with an appropriate excuse in time.

"You find him interesting! I don't believe it," Angela exclaimed. "For ten years you haven't seriously looked at a man. Then you run one down in a dash for your truck and you fall for him?"

Samantha scowled. "Very funny."

"You actually brought him here, you talked with him…."

"For Pete's sake, Angela. I nearly broke his leg!" Samantha looked toward the door, hoping her voice hadn't carried.

Angela simply shook her head, grinning.

"I haven't had time for a man," Samantha interjected, thinking of her grandmother upstairs who, after two strokes, required a part-time nurse to sit with her. All of those expenses demanded that Samantha run a successful business.

"You should be married by now," Angela said dreamily.

Samantha rolled her eyes. "Spare me your adolescent ideas of love. I haven't had time for a man."

"Hey, all of my uncles are married and my dad—"

Samantha sighed. "One day, maybe. It's not that I don't want to be married...." She thought again of her grandmother, the shape the store was in, and then shook her head.

"Our guest needs ice."

Angela continued to grin. Twisting the cap on the ice bag she patted the bottom to make sure it was secure. "This conversation isn't over," Angela warned before leaving.

How well Samantha knew that. This conversation was far from over. Angela wouldn't rest until she'd heard every detail. The woman had too much imagination and too much time—a dangerous combination.

Still, Angela was her dearest friend, closer than a sister, the only real family she had. She could forgive Angela anything. She would do anything for her, too.

Samantha quickly slipped into the main part of the kitchen and set to work fixing up a tray of

treats and hot drinks. She could hear Angela talking to the man in the main room.

The deep timbre of his voice as he answered
floated gently back into the kitchen, surrounding
her with such peace. How long had it been since
she'd been so at peace? His voice invited rest. The
sure, soothing tones made her think he was a man
well in control of himself at all times. How she
wished she had a bit of that control. It'd be nice
to have it in her business. Unfortunately, she
wasn't a good businessperson, though she dearly
loved to create the recipes her grandmother had
made. Instead, she was watching the business
slide further and further toward bankruptcy, toward the end of an era, a way of carrying on her
family's tradition through her recipes. She'd been
so used to working, trying to make this store a
success, that she'd forgotten the joy of simply being in the company of a man—especially a man
who radiated such gentleness. What would it be
like to enjoy making the candy again without wor-
rying about overhead and competition and falling
sales?

Lifting the tray, she returned to the main room.
The stranger had removed his coat and was re-

laxed in one of the cushioned chairs, his foot propped up on a stool.

"I hope you don't mind hot chocolate and dark bread."

"Rye?"

She shook her head. "It's a sweet bread." Placing the tray down, she seated herself on the old-fashioned sofa. She couldn't help but notice how well the charcoal-gray suit fit him. It looked tailor-made, curving over his shoulders, tapering in at the waist, buttoning over his flat stomach.

She realized she was still in her frumpy blue dress and wondered if he noticed how wrinkled it was. She hoped not.

"I was telling Mr. Moore that you've lived here most of your life."

Angela's voice reminded her that she should be serving the company, not staring at him. After cutting a piece of the fresh bread, she handed him a plate and a mug of cocoa.

"You know the town well, then?" he inquired politely.

Samantha nodded. "I suppose so, though I spent most of my time here with my grandmother instead of running around town."

"You enjoy cooking?"

Samantha handed Angela a cup and then picked up her own mug. "I enjoyed being with my grandmother who enjoyed cooking and passed the skill on to me."

"I like to cook as well," he commented, and took a sip of the cocoa.

Surprised, Samantha paused, cocoa halfway to her lips. "Really?"

"Cinnamon and…" he paused, his gaze drifting. "Hazelnut? Freshly ground?"

"How'd you know that?" she asked, stunned.

His gaze refocused on her. "I apologize, Miss Hampton. As I said, I enjoy cooking and have spent years at it."

"It's Samantha. May I ask if you're a chef?" Samantha found it hard to believe she'd found a man interested in cooking.

Richard Moore's gaze turned to his cup. "No. I'm not really a chef. At one time, perhaps, but no more." He swirled the contents before taking another sip. "Now I do a bit of everything, I suppose."

"Is that why you're here? To find a job?" Angela interjected, leaning forward, her golden hair slipping over her shoulder before she brushed it back. Angela was full of energy and curiosity this evening, Samantha thought, but didn't try to quell her. She wanted to know the answer to that question, too.

"Actually, yes. I'm from out of town and just arrived to work at a new store in the mall that's going up."

"I love the mall going in. I've met so many new people—some with accents like yours. Do you know, the guy who runs the Mexican restaurant is from Zimbabwe! And then there is the woman who sounds French but is really from Louisiana and is Cajun, like a relative of mine— the Cajun works as a waitress there. And this guy who owns a shoe store has an accent just like yours, and then—"

"Angela," Samantha said politely.

Angela looked a bit guilty for running on, but that didn't stop her. "So, have you found a place to live yet?"

"Angela," Samantha warned, beginning to feel embarrassed at Angela's persistence in ferreting out all of Mr. Moore's secrets. "He might not want to tell us everything."

"It's not a secret," her guest said, but Samantha had just the opposite feeling.

The muted emotions in the man's dark eyes

made her wonder if he really didn't enjoy talking about himself at all. Angela, however, didn't seem to notice the sudden reserve in his demeanor as he continued.

"I'm living in a nearby hotel until I find an apartment to rent."

"Which will take longer now that you can't walk on your foot."

Samantha turned three shades of red. "Angela!"

"What?" she asked, her eyes all wide and innocent—too innocent.

Samantha's gaze narrowed.

"Your employer didn't mean to run me over, Angela," he chided gently. "It's not her fault I can't walk."

Angela smiled. "Of course it is. She as much as admitted it to me in the supply room—which brings me to my suggestion. You should stay here in the upstairs apartment until you can go house hunting on your own."

Samantha gaped.

Richard gaped as well. Obviously that was not the tack he had expected Angela to take. It hadn't been Samantha's guess either.

"It's perfect," Angela continued. "You need a place to stay and Sam has an empty apartment."

"I—I—" Samantha started.

"Uh-hmm," Richard cleared his throat.

She knew where her friend was headed. Angela had been after her for years to loosen up and date—and she'd just found the perfect candidate.

"I don't want to intrude…" Richard began.

"It's no imposition. Sam really needs to rent out that apartment. Money is tight right now. She could use the rent."

*Please, God, just open a hole in the floor and swallow me up,* she thought dismally.

"Angela!"

Amazingly enough, the man, instead of being shocked, chuckled. "You are a true business-woman, Angela."

His gaze returned to Samantha. "I think your friend has sold me on the idea. However, since you own the apartment, I would think the final decision is up to you. How much do you charge a month?"

Samantha stared at her friend. Rent. Money. That would tide them over, she suddenly realized. At least until February. The firm "no" to renting to this man dissipated before it could be voiced.

Angela named a price.

Samantha started to protest, but Richard nodded. "More than fair for a one-bedroom, one bath."

"Actually, it's a two-bedroom," Samantha interrupted, weakly feeling it best to point that out. This was payback, she thought. It had to be. If she had bowled this man over tonight, she was certainly getting bowled over now, as he and Angela made plans about the apartment before she could comment one way or another.

His warm gaze returned to her, making her forget that she'd even entertained such an idea as payback. That gentle look touched her with acceptance, no hint of her earlier actions in his expression. He really was serious about renting the apartment.

Money.

Maybe God had heard her prayers, after all!

"Even better," Richard added. "Do I get to see it?"

Samantha hesitated. "The service elevator will take you upstairs, but maybe Angela could drive you to pick up your things first so I can do another cleaning before you move in."

Samantha had been using the place for storage

and wanted to move the boxes out. Why hadn't she thought of renting the room before?

He started to protest. She saw the objection in his eyes. Then he nodded.

"However, I insist on taking a cab."

"But..." Angela started.

He shook his head. "The ice has really helped. I can hobble back to the hotel and pack my things. What about picking up the keys tomorrow?"

Samantha thought that sounded superb. She nodded. "I— Wow." She sighed.

Angela chuckled. "God answers prayers, Mr. Moore. Do you believe that?"

Richard smiled at Samantha, his eyes gleaming with amusement. "I do—now."

She had no idea what he meant by that. She did, however, know what her friend meant. With a short warning glare at Angela, she stood.

"Let me get you a cane to at least help you, Mr. Moore. Then we'll see to your cab." She paused. "I can't apologize enough for what happened this evening."

His gaze met hers firmly and he replied, so sure of himself that it sent chills down her spine.

"And I can't thank you enough. If you hadn't

run into me, I might not have met you. And that would have been the greater accident.''

She hesitated at that accent of his, thinking how absolutely appealing it was. Shaking her head, she smiled. "The apartment. Of course. Yes. You found an apartment."

And before he could contradict her, Samantha fled back to the supply room to find her grandmother's walking cane.

Just when things had looked dismal, God had answered her prayers.

The sound of firecrackers outside told her it must be midnight. A new year and a new day.

# Chapter Three

Dillon Sandal stared at his friend. "You're what?"

Richard zipped closed his garment bag and carefully turned. "I've rented an apartment and I'm taking a few weeks off."

Dillon ran a hand through his jet-black hair, exasperation clear in his action. "You just got here. How did you find an apartment so quickly? No, wait. First, answer what happened to your foot."

Dillon strode forward, jerked the garment bag from his friend's hands and carried it over to where Richard's other suitcases sat.

Richard shrugged. Shifting the crutches under his arms he replied, "I broke my ankle."

Richard had gone home, but, unable to sleep because of the pain, he had finally admitted defeat and gone to the emergency room. Surprisingly, one of the ankle bones had a hairline fracture. Samantha was going to love that, he thought ruefully. He probably wouldn't live it down.

"Why didn't you call me? I would have taken you to the hospital. When I left you last night, you were in here, alone."

He paced back to his friend. "I come here this morning to find you packing, and in a partial cast, no less, talking about renting an apartment. And now you're taking a bit of extra time off—"

"You should be glad. That means you'll get to run everything until I recover."

"I run everything anyway," Dillon muttered. Dillon and Richard had gone to college together. Dillon was the one close friend Richard had.

Whenever a new store opened, Dillon took on the role of manager to oversee the hiring and ensure a smooth transition as it took place in the community. Richard usually came to make sure publicity was seen to, as well as a million and one other things. After all, he was being groomed to take over the business one day. His father thought he should know each store personally. So, while his maternal grandfather was the figurehead appearing in most of the commercials and interviews, and his da was the CEO who ran things now, Richard was left as the man behind the scenes doing the legwork for all the store openings.

Dillon dropped into one of the chairs and crossed his khaki-covered legs.

With his green polo shirt and dark brown loafers, Dillon looked like a young executive ready for the golf course. Of course, Richard knew Dillon preferred to dress that way, leaving the business suits to him. Still, he admired how relaxed his friend looked in the luxury room.

"So, what really happened to your foot?" Dillon asked.

Richard sighed and hobbled over to the edge of the frilly-lace-covered bed of the hotel and sat. While they waited for someone to climb the old-fashioned staircase to get his luggage he said, "I told you. I fell."

"The rest of the story," Dillon prodded.

Richard allowed his head to drop back. Staring at the stucco ceiling, he debated how best to answer. His eyes wandered to the cherry-wood posters that were draped with a thin see-through lacy thing and thought this was definitely a room for a girl. Even the chairs and tables had lacy stuff on them. He wasn't going to miss the decor at all.

"I decided to go to a special midnight service at one of the local churches," he finally said, returning his gaze to his friend.

Both eyebrows shot up as Dillon stared. "Really?"

Richard nodded and shifted on the down-filled bedspread. "No one knows me here. I wouldn't be hounded."

Dillon shook his head. "You are hounded back in New York because of the places you go, my friend. If you'd find a smaller church, like mine, or avoid—"

"Like my father would allow that?" Richard interrupted. "I am the business's future," he said wearily. "I have to go to all of those functions whenever I'm home." He'd been through this with Dillon too many times to count.

Dillon shook his head. "You should talk to your father, tell him you're not happy doing this."

Richard sighed. "What else would I do? I've trained for this my entire life."

He didn't like the sympathetic look his friend shot him. Talking about his accident, although he knew his friend was going to rib him, was better than dealing with that look. So, taking a breath he said, "I was running late and hurrying toward the church when this woman came rushing out and knocked me flat."

It took Dillon a moment to change gears. When he did, his jaw dropped. Slowly a half smile curved his lips. Disbelief filled his eyes. "A woman did this?" He motioned toward Richard's foot.

There it was. He'd had it now. Richard nodded, glancing out the window. A weak sun shone through the white lacy curtains, indicating that there was still the possibility of snow. "Yeah. She'd forgotten her purse in her truck and was hurrying to get it. It was dark out and I guess she didn't see me."

"Didn't see you?" he parroted, laughter filling his voice. "A woman didn't notice you? She was driving a *truck?*" Dillon's voice rose.

Restrained no more, his laughter burst into the room, filling every silent corner as it reverberated off the walls. Throwing his head back, he dropped his other foot to the floor and guffawed loud and long.

"It's not that humorous, dear fellow," Richard murmured.

His accent only sent Dillon into a fresh round of laughter. "Obviously it is, if you've lapsed back into that British brogue."

"I'm Irish," Richard reminded him, irked that Dillon was getting such a kick out of this.

"Let me guess, five foot ten inches, two hundred pounds of muscle, and her name is Frieda. She wears jeans and a flannel shirt, chews tobacco and looks as mean as a coyote fighting over his newest meal?"

Unruffled by this latest round of insults from his friend, Richard smiled. "You'd be wrong in your guess."

"Oh yeah?" Dillon challenged.

A knock at the door interrupted them. Thank goodness.

"Get that," Richard interjected, ignoring the question in Dillon's voice.

Dillon rose and opened the door to the bellhop. Young, no more than twenty, the boy had outgrown the outfit he wore. The sleeves and pants were both just a tad too short and a bit too tight. However, what he lacked in the uniform, he certainly made up with the smile he gave them.

"Ready to go?" he drawled.

"Can you put these in the silver Lexus out front?" Dillon asked.

"Yes, sir," the boy answered. He quickly and quietly started gathering Richard's luggage, full of as much energy as a young man could be who was out making a living at a job he enjoyed. Where had Richard's energy for his job gone lately?

Turning back to Richard, Dillon said, "So, when do I get to know where you're moving?"

Richard pushed himself up onto his good leg. Today he wore his own pair of khakis with a long-sleeved white shirt. A loose tweed sports jacket finished out his outfit. Slipping on his tanned overcoat, he left it unbuckled and unbuttoned as he grabbed his crutches. "Since you're driving me there, I suppose you can know now."

Adjusting the crutches, he matched his gait to the swing of the metal devices as he maneuvered his way out the door. "There's a tiny shop two blocks from the mall that is renting out a flat."

"Wow. That's close."

Richard nodded. "Quite. I plan to reside there in peace for at least the next four weeks until this foot heals. Then I'll return to work."

Dillon fell in beside his friend. "Four weeks. What about the grand opening of the store?"

Richard frowned. "We can push it off for a month if we must. Maybe plan it for Valentine's Day. After all, that would be a great time for the opening."

"You know, you're right." Dillon's mind clicked into motion. "We could do a huge campaign and build up to the grand opening targeting Valentine's Day. Of course, we don't want to forget to play up that this is the one hundredth store in America. I'm sure we could pull a lot of people from Amarillo and maybe even the Fort Worth and Dallas area if the advertising campaign were big enough. But that's your department. I have some ideas for inside the store. I think you're going to enjoy what I have planned."

Richard nodded. "I'll be glad to look it over, but do me a favor."

"What's that?" Dillon asked as they approached the stairs.

Richard turned slightly and oh-so-carefully began descending. "I don't want to discuss business when I'm around anyone else. I want four weeks of rest, pure and simple. I want only to experience life in this little town and have time to recuperate.''

''From Linda,'' Dillon said knowingly.

''Not just from Linda, but from society.''

His fiancée of four years had left him six months ago. He'd found out she was leaving him by the announcement in the *New York Times* about her upcoming marriage—to someone else.

He was embarrassed to admit he'd been so busy that he hadn't even realized the woman he'd agreed to marry four years earlier had fallen for another man. That still smarted.

Since then, however, he'd been taking stock of his life. The store was all he'd ever had, all he ever would have. He'd been so caught up in the business, he realized now, that he and Linda hadn't really had a conventional relationship. He'd met her at a few parties. His father, he now understood, had manipulated things so he and Linda were together—with Linda's full support— and it had just seemed natural to ask her to marry him. It had been just like a business merger. She was a society woman and knew how things worked. He was going to be in that type of spotlight. He'd thought, sure, why not.

He knew when he read the announcement and felt only embarrassment that he hadn't really loved Linda. She was manipulative and only wanted what his father had promised her—a name and place in society.

But that incident had gotten Richard to thinking about life. Church last night had been part of the new leaf he was going to turn over. He had decided that he had to get back to basics to find out just who and what he was.

God was as basic as he could get. He needed to reestablish that relationship and then go from there.

He was at a crossroads.

"Richard?" Dillon prompted, and he realized he hadn't answered him.

"Linda is part of the reason I don't want to talk about work. Truthfully, buddy, I simply need time. And this store, so far away from New York, gives me a chance to do some reevaluating."

His friend nodded. "Very well. I'll do my best to take my lead from you about work discussions."

"I plan to have a line installed in the apartment

and a fax put in. If any emergencies arise, you
can contact me there or on my cell.''

Dillon pursed his lips. ''You're really serious
about this.''

He nodded. ''I am.''

They reached the bottom of the wooden stairs.
The bellboy was just coming back in and paused
to hold the door open. Richard reached into his
front pocket and pulled out his money clip. Peel-
ing off two bills, he gave the young man a nice
tip and nodded.

''Thank *you,* sir,'' the boy said, and smiled.

Richard smiled in return. Evidently, the tip he'd
normally leave in New York was considered
much better here.

Going out into the windy morning air, he
wished he'd at least buckled his coat.

''So, then,'' Dillon continued as the door
closed behind him. ''Tell me about this apartment.''

Richard got to the luxury car and handed the
crutches to his friend. Grabbing the door and the
top of the car he lowered himself into the front
passenger's seat. Carefully he lifted his leg and
turned, working it into the car while avoiding
bumping it.

When the car was in gear and they were carefully headed down the icy, sand- and salt-coated roads, Richard said, "I've never seen the apartment."

Both hands on the wheel, Dillon cast him a quick look. "You're kidding."

"The woman told me there was a two-bedroom apartment for rent. I agreed."

"That's not practical. What if it's a broken-down heap?"

"What if it is?" Richard replied. "I'm only going to be there for a few weeks. It's away from the places I would normally stay and it'll give me some peace and quiet."

Dillon frowned. "You're willing to risk renting an apartment unseen, just for peace and quiet? I don't buy it."

"Turn here," Richard said, pointing to the main east-to-west street.

Dillon obediently obeyed.

"See that gingerbread house toward the end of the block?" he continued, pointing. "Right past the hardware store?"

"Yeah."

"Just after there you'll turn into the alley."

Dillon started, "You're—"

"—kidding," Richard finished for him. "No, I'm not."

Main Street was nothing like a main street in New York. Here, lining the straight four-lane street, were metered parking spaces. Down the middle of the street—though not up farther, he'd noted—was a median filled with grass and benches. There were flower beds but they were empty right now. He imagined this was a very beautiful area in the spring. A big clock stood on the corner, right beyond the hardware store and the candy store.

At the corner they turned right and then made another quick right. The alley was clean and wide enough for two cars, though it'd be a tight fit. Dumpsters sat behind the stores, most likely an indication that the garbage trucks made this their route to collect trash.

"Though there is a side entrance, I thought it'd be better to unload everything back here. I called and talked to one of the workers this morning, who told me this would be best."

"Wait a minute," Dillon said, his mind working furiously as he processed everything. "You're staying at this candy shop?"

Richard buckled his coat and then shoved the

car door open. "They have an apartment for rent."

"But don't you think staying under the competition's roof—"

"She's not our competition," Richard said shortly.

Dillon's eyebrows shot up. Quickly, he exited the car. "She? She?" He spied a red truck next to the building. His gaze returned to Richard. "The woman who hit you offered you a place to stay?"

He should have realized Dillon would put two and two together.

When he opened the trunk, Richard grabbed the smaller of the two suitcases, leaving the large one as well as the garment bag for his friend, and went to the back door to ring the bell.

The door was opened by Angela.

"Oh, great! You made it."

"Young and fresh is now your style?" Dillon said through the side of his mouth as the woman pulled the door wider.

"Can it," Richard replied.

"You're on crutches. Sam is going to absolutely die!" the young girl said with glee.

"Sam?" Dillon asked.

"Hi. I'm Angela." She stuck out her hand, saw his were filled and dropped her hand to her side. "Sam is the one who broke his ankle. It is broken, isn't it? I told Sam it was."

Richard sighed and entered the building. "Yes, it's broken."

The small entryway was brightly lit by fluorescent lights. He saw a table and desk along with two chairs, and stairs and an old elevator. This must be the other side of the elevator doors he'd seen last night.

"Yes! I knew it!" Angela said, pumping her hand in the air.

"You're glad he has a broken ankle?" Dillon asked.

Richard was a bit amazed at the woman's attitude as well.

"Oh. No. Of course not." She blushed. "I'm getting my vet's license and my uncle and aunt are doctors, and I bet Sam she'd broken that ankle from the way it looked. I was right, so I don't have to clean up at closing today."

Richard shook his head.

"You're impudent," Dillon said superiorly.

"Wow. I'm impressed. Someone who knows how to read a dictionary."

Dillon's jaw dropped.

Clearing his throat, he asked, "Can someone show me where the apartment is?"

Without a word Angela turned and hurried to the elevator.

The doors slid open and that's when Richard's secret for staying here was revealed. On the other side of the elevator, those doors had slid open as well, and there stood Samantha, but not Samantha from the night before. This Samantha was wearing jeans and a soft blue cashmere pullover. And in front of her was an older woman with white hair pulled up into a bun who sat in a wheelchair.

"Good morning," Samantha said to them.

Realizing the breach of manners, Richard cleared his throat. "Good morning, Sam. As you can see, I'm here to take possession of my flat."

He saw the look Dillon was giving him and ignored it. "This is my friend I spoke of last evening—Dillon Sandal."

She nodded. "Nice to meet you. I was just taking Granny up for her morning physical therapy. The nurse should be here soon."

They all entered the elevator.

Five people and three pieces of luggage, not to mention a wheelchair and crutches, made for a crowded fit. Richard scooted until he was next to Samantha.

"Well," Dillon said as the door closed.

That was it. Just "well." He was speechless, it seemed.

Which was fine with Richard.

As the elevator jerked into motion Richard caught a whiff of the sweet aroma of cinnamon. It came from Samantha.

"He broke his ankle!"

Leave it to Angela to break the silence.

"What?" Samantha gasped. Her gaze, which had touched only briefly on Dillon and him, had been mainly on the woman in the chair. It now dropped to Richard's ankle, which had been blocked by Dillon when the elevator opened, and she cringed.

Feeling a tug on his pants, he looked down to see that the grandmother had hold of him. She jerked on his trouser leg, then patted his thigh.

His eyes widened.

"What is it, Granny?" Samantha asked, seeing the action too.

"Granny" jerked again at his trousers and patted his thigh.

He felt his cheeks actually heating. Obviously, she didn't have all of her faculties.

"I don't understand," Samantha said, and listened as the old woman gurgled out something that sound like "rush" and then "done."

Thankfully the doors opened.

Samantha glanced up, harried. "Is your ankle really broken— Just a minute, Granny— Oh!" She shook her head. "I'll talk to you later. Angie, show him the apartment and make sure he has a key to the side and back doors."

She exited the elevator and headed off down the hall.

"This way," Angela said, going in the opposite direction.

"Wow." Dillon shook his head and followed the young woman.

Richard only cleared his throat again, adjusted the crutches and then did the same. "I'd say," he finally added as they started down the hall. "Is that type of incident normal for Granny?" Richard asked Angela as they slowly made their way around the corner and down the hall to one of the apartments located there.

"Oh, no. She's smart as a whip. I'm not sure what was up with your pants, though." Angie laughed. "This first apartment is mine. The one down here is yours. Sam has one apartment on the other side of the elevator and Granny has the other."

"You and *Sam* are related?" Dillon asked.

"No. Everyone calls Sam's grandmother Granny. Probably because that's what Sam calls her. She's a nice old lady. You'll get used to seeing her around. She'll be down there later today while we work. She usually sits in the living room during the afternoon and watches TV or reads. We have a communal living room and dining area downstairs. The kitchen too. Of course, there are separate ones up here and sometimes I eat up here, but usually we all just gather down in the main room in the evening. When Granny converted this building into apartments years ago, she left the main living room intact so that there would always be a gathering place for company and such."

Dillon nodded.

"Here we go." Angela opened the door. Turning, she handed the key to Richard. "I'll go get you the other keys. In the meantime, enjoy." She trotted off down the hall.

As soon as she was gone, Dillon turned to Richard. "Sam is the one who ran you down?"

Richard shrugged, a small smile on his face.

Dillon shook his head. "Boy, you've got it bad."

Richard didn't know if he agreed with his friend's assessment, but he would enjoy finding out just what he "had" while he worked on discovering what life was all about.

He glanced around the room, dropping his suitcase near the sofa. He walked over and looked out the window before returning to the sofa.

"I'll drop these in your bedroom," Dillon said, and headed off down the hall with the luggage.

"I'm going to make some calls," Richard said, and pulled out his cell phone, intending to call the phone company.

Before he could get settled, however, Samantha tapped on the door.

Dillon, who was just coming up the hall into the living room, grinned knowingly at his friend.

"Come in," Richard offered.

Samantha entered.

"Dillon was just leaving," Richard said.

Dillon lifted an eyebrow but took the hint.

"Oh, I don't want to run anyone off," Samantha protested.

"You aren't," Dillon said, and cast a look at his friend that said *we'll talk later.* "I need to get going."

He scooted past her out the door.

Samantha clasped her hands.

Silence fell.

Richard snapped his cell phone closed and dropped onto the sofa.

"I was just planning to get comfortable. Won't you have a seat?"

She shook her head. "No. I just wanted to apologize for Granny."

"For what?" Richard asked curiously. Shifting, he lifted his foot and rested it on the coffee table in front of him.

Samantha hesitated and then closed the door behind her. She crossed the room and braced her hands on the back of an overstuffed chair, as if keeping that between them would somehow protect her.

"Granny is very peculiar sometimes. But I don't think I've ever seen her pulling on someone like that. She's old...."

Richard motioned to Samantha. "Please, come sit here." He patted the sofa next to him.

Reluctantly, she came from behind the chair and, after a moment's hesitation, dropped down on the sofa. Richard reached out and took her hand. "Sam," he said gently, "this has been a wild meeting for both of us. Heaping guilt for imagined offenses isn't going to help either one of us."

Samantha's gaze skittered away.

Her hand felt good in his. He normally was not so forward, but there was something about this woman.

Finally, her gaze returned to his. "I can suggest a doctor if the ER doctor hasn't assigned you one."

Richard chuckled.

Samantha blushed. "I—"

"No, no. Don't apologize." He knew she was about to apologize again. "I'll be glad for the suggestion. The ER doctor wants me to find one and have a checkup on this." He finally released her hand. "But in the meantime, why don't you simply relax? I don't have to see another doctor for a few days, and I think it'd be nice if we started over—getting to know each other, that is."

Samantha hesitated again and then nodded. "That sounds great."

She stood.

Richard felt a loss, but allowed her to go by saying, "I've got some unpacking to do, so perhaps I'll see you later."

"I'll be downstairs working," she replied, and headed to the door.

"Goodbye," he said softly.

"Goodbye."

As the door closed, he admitted that Dillon was right. He did have it bad.

But was that really so wrong?

# Chapter Four

"Boy, do you have it bad."

"Have what?" Samantha said to Angela as she headed into the professional kitchen to start on a batch of caramel-filled chocolate drops. She'd been working on them before Granny's physical therapist arrived.

"You know." Angela pointed her index finger toward the upstairs.

Samantha rolled her eyes. "Please spare me. I don't have time to worry about my boarder. I've got candy to make."

Samantha swiped a strand of hair back out of her face and started mixing the ingredients. She had been harried this morning, trying to get caught up on everything. Taking her grandmother up to the therapist had actually been a bonus as she'd gotten to chat some with her new boarder.

Except that when he'd taken her hand she hadn't thought of him as a boarder at all, but as a very eligible male who was too handsome for his own good and too forgiving.

Of course, that could be good. She'd longed for a break from work, from the pressures of thinking about the business, and he certainly was providing it.

"He didn't tell me how badly he broke his ankle," Angela said, her mind, while on the upstairs guest, definitely on a different track than Samantha's.

Samantha was more interested in their upstairs company than she liked to admit however, so she said simply, "I'll have to cut his rent or something for what happened."

"No, you won't."

Samantha jumped and spun around. Standing in the doorway was the object of their discussion.

Wow, did he look good. The tweed jacket he wore stretched across those wide shoulders, making him look like a linebacker. His waist, however, was small and trim. He was older than she was. How did he do it? She struggled every day to keep her figure and yet this man looked as if he never had a problem looking perfect.

"I didn't see you there," Angela said and, flushing at being caught talking about him, scooted out toward the front of the store.

"I thought you were unpacking."

"I decided to do it later," he murmured. "There were some other things I wanted to do first."

Samantha watched Angela leave and realized, disgustedly, that someone was matchmaking. It was one thing for Samantha to think about it, but for Angela to scheme...

"Did you ever think that if I hadn't been day-dreaming I might have seen you coming?"

Surprised, she paused with the sugar in her hands. "Daydreaming?" Her gaze studied the man who leaned so carefully on his crutches.

He chuckled at her look. "Is it that hard to imagine?"

"I just—" She shook her head and finished pouring the ingredients in before turning on the mixing machine. She couldn't tell him he looked so together that he didn't seem the type to daydream. Still, that one word aroused her curiosity. "About what?"

She shouldn't have asked, but maybe Angela's boldness was wearing off on her.

Richard took that as an invitation to come in. He slowly made his way across the floor until he was next to her, and replied. "About this town. Small-town life. I was wondering just how nice it would be to find a small town like this, settle down and not be on the move constantly."

"Oh." He smelled fresh and slightly musky. She tried to place the scent of his cologne, but it eluded her. She found herself wanting to lean in and take another sniff.

How long had it been since she'd met a man who cared about his appearance, smelled so good and was single? Now Mitch, Angela's uncle, he always smelled great, but he was married to Suzi and had three children. Then there was his older brother, Zach. He had a rustic outdoorsy smell, and a person could never miss him with that cowboy hat of his constantly perched on his head. And he always had Laura on his arm or their daughter by the hand. He was often in here buying her or their daughter something.

Mark, Laura's brother, was a smart dresser and

had that Cajun accent, and, boy, was he something—but he was married to Leah.

All of the good ones in town were married, except Liam and now this man. Of course, as far as Samantha was concerned, Liam was a troublemaker who hadn't gotten caught yet. And if he didn't stop sniffing around Angela, Mitch was going to make sure he caught Liam at something. She ought to mention it to his brother Drake, who was also married. He came in occasionally with his walker or cane, according to how the weather was affecting his old injuries.

Glancing up, she suddenly realized that none of the guys who came in buying gifts for their wives were quite as handsome as this man next to her. *Rugged* didn't fit him, nor did *elegant*.

*Old World.*

Yeah, that was it. Since he came from somewhere over there. Maybe England?

She wondered if he knew those shoe people moving into the mall down the street, then scoffed at that. They had many foreign people in their growing town. Just look at the Dunnington's store—though she doubted they had anyone from New York down here. She wasn't sure exactly how chain stores worked. The national chain shoe store certainly wasn't a British store, but a British man ran it.

The fact she was from America didn't mean she knew the Kennedys or the President of the United States. Shoot, she didn't even know everyone in Hill Creek! So, why would he know any of the foreign people who worked in the mall?

*Okay, calm down,* she told herself silently. *You always do this when you get nervous.*

"I dream too," she said now, turning back to her candy. "But in my dreams it's simply keeping my head above water and seeing this store a success once again."

"Troubles?"

Her eyes widened in dismay. "I can't believe I said that out loud!"

With consternation she realized her cheeks were heating up.

Politely he turned his attention to the candy making. "I love cooking, though I rarely make candy. Cookies, main dishes, more exotic things."

"A connoisseur?"

"No. It's a pastime. I enjoy cooking and have picked up ideas from all the different countries I've visited."

"You travel a lot?"

He smiled. "I grew up in schools in England. Our countries are much different from yours. They're all much smaller, so traveling is much cheaper and much easier."

"Why did you come to America?"

"For college. And now I travel for business."

"To Hill Creek?" Samantha asked, shaking her head.

"I do publicity for big openings." He pulled a roll of mints out of his pocket and peeled back the paper to pop one in his mouth.

*Aha,* thought Samantha. "And this mall is one of those things." She sighed. "I doubt you're interested, but I'm planning to do a huge publicity push for Valentine's Day for my store."

Richard coughed and grabbed at his throat, choking on the mint.

Samantha glanced up at him. His face had turned red as he tried to clear his airway.

"Are you okay?"

Quickly abandoning her job, she crossed to the sink and grabbed a glass from the cabinet next to it. Going to the refrigerator she jerked open the freezer portion, snatched some ice and dropped it into the glass. She sloshed some water into the container from the faucet and then returned to his side.

The coughing had subsided, though he still cleared his throat as if hurting from the mint that had gone down the wrong way.

He accepted it and took a sip. "Valentine's Day, you say?"

"Yeah." Sighing, she gave up and confessed, "The store isn't doing well. It's been going slowly downhill since Granny had one of her strokes five years ago. But now, with this superstore moving in down the street, I'm afraid we're not going to make it. Angie and I were talking. If we do a big buildup for Valentine's Day, we're hoping to start increasing our market once again. We're hoping the other store isn't opening until March or so, then we'll get the Valentine's Day crowd."

Peering intently at Richard, she said, "Are you feeling ill?"

"I, uh, actually think I should be sitting down."

"Oh dear." Samantha again abandoned her post and slipped her arm behind Richard. "Let's go into the living room. I'm so sorry. This is all my fault."

"No. No, it's not." He grabbed Samantha's hands, stopping her in her tracks. "You shouldn't be feeling guilty for any of this. Remember, we're starting over."

She sighed. It was her nature to feel guilty. But he was right. She glanced up at him. "It's going to be hard to let go of that habit."

"Well, let's start with me, then. You can practice letting go by repeating, 'I am not at fault.'"

"I am not at fault," she mimicked.

"Good," he murmured.

Their eyes met and held before he finally released her hands. "I should let you get back to cooking."

"Oh yeah." She nodded.

He nodded.

"If you'll excuse me, I need to call Dillon."

Samantha said quickly, "I hope you'll join us later for dinner."

She had the distinct feeling he was trying to get away from her. Was it because he knew she was having business problems? She shouldn't have admitted so much.

Or maybe he realized she was attracted to him. He was a world traveler. She was just a working girl from a tiny town who didn't know up from down sometimes.

Nibbling her lip she watched as he stood and slipped the crutches under his arms. "That sounds nice," he said in that beautiful voice of his. "Until then."

He turned and slowly made his way out of the living room and through the kitchen toward the back of the house. He was going out.

He'd be there for dinner.

That was good, wasn't it? Or was he just being nice? she wondered, wringing her hands.

Oh heavens, she'd just promised the man she wouldn't blame herself. And here she was, doing it again.

He was just moving in, for Pete's sake. He had to go run errands.

He was her boarder!

The sound of her mixer stopping warned her it was time to change machines. With a heavy sigh she hurried back into the kitchen, wondering if this renter was going to last the week or if she'd scared him off.

"Thanks, Dad," she said out loud. "If I could get over your leaving, perhaps I might not be so paranoid about every other person I meet leaving me too.''

Thinking back to the handsome man, she said again, ''I am not at fault. I am not at fault. I am not... I wonder if he's single.''

Yeah, she had it bad.

# *Chapter Five*

It only took one hour for Dillon to get his message and return to Richard's apartment. Richard had just collapsed on the fifties-style sofa and propped his injured foot up on the antique oak coffee table when Dillon walked into the apartment.

"Thanks for knocking," Richard drawled, as Dillon strode across the room.

Dillon shrugged. "We've shared too many hotel rooms and dorm rooms for me to worry about that. Now, what is so important that I had to come right back over here? And, by the way, you look like death."

Richard grimaced. "I had no idea a pair of

crutches could wear a person out. My arms are stiff and sore, my back feels like matchsticks that have been broken, and my hip, well, we'll leave it at that.'' He rubbed his hip gingerly.

"What have you been doing, aerobics?'' He sniffed toward Richard as if trying to see if he smelled.

"I was hanging up my clothes. Back and forth. Back and forth.'' He waved toward the bedroom.

"It could have waited,'' Dillon replied mildly, taking a seat in one of the two armchairs.

Richard shrugged. "Perhaps, but it is best to get these things done and out of the way.''

"There goes the accent again, bud. So, why don't you tell me what's really up?'' Dillon propped his feet, too, on the coffee table.

Richard sighed. His friend knew him too well. And he knew Dillon just as well—well enough to know that he wasn't going to be happy with what Richard was about to say. "We need to change the big opening day at the store from Valentine's Day to something like July Fourth.''

Dillon's jaw dropped. "You're kidding, right?''

"You say that too much,'' Richard said.

Dillon straightened in his chair, disbelief on his

face. "Dick, my boy, I just spent the last hour on the phone with the home office getting everything arranged."

Richard scowled at the shortening of his name. He really hated it when people did that, and Dillon knew that. What bothered him even more was that Dillon had already put the ball in motion. He had hoped, just possibly, Dillon hadn't made any calls yet.

He felt a sinking sensation.

"You wouldn't want to call them back and change it to the Fourth of July?"

A short bark of laughter escaped Dillon. Resting his right ankle atop his left leg, he said, "Are you serious? I had to speak with your father over this change of plans. He wasn't happy, especially when I mentioned you needed the time off because of an accident. But I convinced him this would really work out better. Opening February tenth, the Thursday before Valentine's Day, would make a wonderful campaign. Once he warmed up to the idea he acted like he might even promote me."

"You're directly underneath me," Richard said.

Dillon grinned. "Yeah, I know. You didn't

know I was bucking for your job, did you," he joked. "Seriously, though, your dad was very happy and decided this was a great move. Do you really think I can call him back now and ask him to change it? You know these openings are usually set in stone per your father's orders."

"Maybe I should call him," Richard murmured.

Dillon's eyebrows shot up. "I won't say it, but...yes, I will. Think of how that'd make me look. Think how it'd tick off your dad. You really don't want to upset him now. Not after the Linda fiasco."

Richard sighed. Dillon was right. It'd chop Dillon's feet right out from under him if he called his dad up and said he didn't want the store opening on Valentine's Day. It would also be a bad business move.

Yeah, his dad would be upset. His dad was still upset that he'd "let Linda get away."

"Just what is the problem, Richard? And please tell me it doesn't have to do with the woman downstairs."

Richard, who had started to rub the back of his neck, paused and glanced at his friend.

"Oh, this is just great." Dillon dropped both

feet to the ground and stood. Striding across the room to the tall oblong window, he looked out at the blustery January day. He shoved his hands onto his trim hips and turned around. "I knew she was trouble the minute I saw her. I knew it. The look in your eyes. I've never seen that look before. I said, Dillon. Dillon, this girl spells trouble. She sure does. If she can distract Richard from work and even get Mr. Hotel-mania to move into an apartment, then we have a major problem here." He shook his head. Reaching up, he shoved aside one of the long curtains that hung open, unpinned, in front of the window. "What'd she do when she knocked you down, Richard? Did she crack that head of yours?"

Dillon turned back around and strode across the room as if to look at Richard's head.

Richard held up a hand. "That's quite enough."

Dillon dropped back into the wing-backed paisley brocade chair. Thumping the wood that decorated the arm with his fingers, he said, "What has happened in the last twenty-four hours, Richard?"

That was the first serious question Richard had heard since Dillon had walked in. Richard owed his friend an answer. But what did he want to answer? His entire life had been skewered out of control, or perhaps for the first time in months, on track.

"I think when Samantha knocked me to the ground last night, she must have finally knocked some sense into me."

Dillon blew out a breath in disgust. Ah well, Richard thought, he'd come around if he explained a bit more.

"I know it's crazy, but when I was laying there and finally focused on her eyes...Dillon, it was like I had come home, like I had found something I was missing."

Richard shifted in his chair, uncomfortable with being so honest. "I am tired of the nightlife and the life I'm expected to lead. Finding out my fiancée was actually engaged to someone else was a wake-up call. It got me to thinking—in New York, Dillon, not here, but in New York. I started wondering what had happened to my life. In the past five years I have been running so hard that part of me got lost somewhere along the way. Oh, I go through the motions. I go to work, go to fund-raisers and parties and the occasional church function.

"But what has happened to my spiritual life? I was thinking just last week that I couldn't remember the last time I prayed. I didn't remember the last time I cracked open my Bible. I couldn't remember the last time I sat by the fire with my grandda and simply talked about God. You know, he's the one who led me to the Lord when I was home in Ireland one summer twenty years ago."

Richard remembered the conversation and the fervency he'd had for God. There had been such joy and peace in his heart. He'd rushed to church every Sunday, wanting to devour what they had waiting for him. Each word that came out of the rector's mouth, Richard had accepted and fed on, digesting it during the week until the next church meeting.

But shortly after college, or maybe even during college, something happened.

He had drifted away.

"What does this have to do with the woman downstairs?"

Richard brought himself back to the present. "I was going to that church, hopefully, to find what I had been missing, but when she knocked me down, I realized that church wasn't the only thing I'd been missing. It was reflected in her eyes. She has a joy for life, for God, for her business. She loves it and is free to express that. Me, I've been so wrapped up in getting things done that I've lost touch with that freedom.''

''It doesn't hurt that she's good-looking either,'' Dillon added wryly.

''I'll admit that I am also very attracted to her. I think—'' Richard broke off.

Dillon's eyes widened at Richard's unspoken implication. ''Oh, no. Don't you dare say it! It's too soon. You only just met her. Remember the fiasco with Linda!''

''What happened with Linda was the right thing to happen, and I'm happy for her.''

''If you could convince your dad of that. He thinks you're still moping.''

Richard shrugged. ''There's a problem, however.''

Dillon groaned. ''Ah. Linda aside, we are finally getting to why you called me over here.''

''Samantha runs a candy shop that deals in homemade candies and her business is in trouble.''

Dillon leaned forward, covering his face with his hands. Oh yes, he knew where this was going,

Richard thought. He could tell by the weary way Dillon rubbed his face.

"Businesses fail every day, Richard."

There was more, however. "She thinks our store has come just to put her out of business."

"No, no, no," Dillon groaned, and rocked back and forth.

"And she has no idea that I'm part of Dunnington's."

"Aargh." Dillon sounded like he was gagging or maybe crying, Richard wasn't sure which.

He waited.

Dillon finally took a deep breath, sat up in the chair and looked right at Richard. "So, tell her who you are."

Richard's heart constricted. "If I do, she's going to think I've purposely deceived her."

"If you don't, she's going to think you've purposely deceived her."

"Therein lies my dilemma."

"So, what are you going to do?" Dillon asked.

Richard sighed. He rubbed a hand down his face. "I don't know. I just don't know. Can you see me going down there and saying, hey, here's your rent money and by the way, I'm the one about to put you out of business?"

"That's not funny, Richard," Dillon said sharply.

"I know it's not, dear boy," Richard said so properly that Dillon groaned again.

Richard sighed.

"You've got to tell her," Dillon finally said, softly.

"I know." Dillon was right. He did have to tell her. And the sooner the better.

"So…?" Dillon prompted.

Richard sighed. "I'll tell her tonight. She's invited me down later for dinner, and I'll find a way to work it into the conversation."

Dillon shook his head. "Better hope that young one isn't around."

"Angela?" Richard asked, surprised.

"Yeah. I have a feeling she'll find a way to get it out of you before you're ready to work it into your chat."

"She is something," Richard said of Angela, and wore the first smile since he had realized just how much Samantha hated Dunnington's.

"Did you find out what was up with the grandmother?" Dillon asked now.

Richard shook his head. "No idea. Angela said

she's smart as a whip. All I can guess is she didn't like my pants.'' He shrugged.

''Samantha is planning to do a major Valentine's Day push to try to get her business up,'' Richard finally added.

''She doesn't have the resources we have,'' Dillon said quietly, realizing just what that meant.

Richard glanced around the small living room area and kitchenette. It was decorated with brocaded furniture that was most likely fifty years old. The bare wood floor had a braided rug on it, and the curtains were well worn but heavy. They would block out the light in the two windows, as well as the one in the bedroom. He'd tested the bed earlier. The mattress was old but still firm and the bed had a beautiful carved headboard.

When he looked around the apartment he realized these were most likely memories for her. He'd bet this had been her mother's or grandmother's furniture at one time and that it had been moved into here just for him, or for someone before him—though, the way she'd acted, he didn't think she had rented this place out lately.

It had a shine, showing the woman had worked hard to clean it before he arrived. That gave him an idea of her character. She was a hard worker who cared about appearances and cared about people.

And his store would most likely put her out of business next month.

Unless…

"Uh-oh. I don't like that look," Dillon said. Warily he sat up straighter, grabbing the arms of the chair.

"I've got an idea."

"You're not calling your dad, are you?"

Richard's lips turned down in a frown. "No. Nothing like that. I'm living here. My money is going to help tide this woman over for the next month and a half as she prepares for the push in her store. What if I simply stay here, listen to what she says and glean some information on how we might be able to help her?"

Dillon blinked. "We're the competition!"

"Be serious, Dillon. This store isn't going to put a dent into our profits. It's a tiny little senti-mental one-man candy factory. If I can stick around, find out just how bad her situation is, I might actually be able to give her some ideas on how to save the store."

"And win her over at the same time."

Richard hesitated. That thought had crossed his

mind. "I'll tell her who I am as soon as the opportunity presents itself. In the meantime, I can help her. Maybe if I'm helping her, she'll realize that I'm not out to destroy her the way she thinks. Then, perhaps, that attraction I saw in her eyes won't go flitting away the minute she finds out who I am."

"I think you're treading on dangerously thin ice, buddy," Dillon said.

"It's the only thing I can think of right now. Go back to the store, do a bit of research on Samantha's business and find out what you can about it. See if you can figure out how we might be able to help them. I'll do the same thing from here."

"If that's what you want," Dillon said in a long-suffering voice that meant he'd accepted Richard's plan but would rather his friend think he still disagreed.

"It is. And thanks. Oh, and Dillon," he said as Dillon rose, "I'm serious about church and God. It's time I got my life back in order. And that's what I am planning on doing, right now."

He pointed to the Bible on the tiny wooden kitchen table.

Dillon followed his gaze. Seeing the Bible, he

got up and strode over to it. He snatched it up, brought it back and dropped it in Richard's lap. ''I think that's a great idea, because when all of this is done, God may be the only one you have left on your side.''

He strode to the door and paused. ''And me, bud.'' Then he walked out, leaving Richard alone in the apartment with only the sound of the high winds occasionally rattling the windowpanes.

Opening his Bible to Romans, Richard began to read.

# Chapter Six

"I'm so glad you could make it for dinner," Samantha said as Richard limped into the room.

Richard smiled. "Thank you for sending Angela up with the reminder. I'd meant to come down earlier but was involved in something else."

Once Richard had started reading his Bible, a hunger that he had forgotten had come over him and he'd found himself wanting to read just one more chapter. Before he'd realized it, he'd read the entire book of Romans. Then, feeling he'd gone through it too quickly, he'd gone back and started over. A small dead part inside him, or what had felt dead, began to grow and glow again.

A peace he'd forgotten began to bubble up inside him, so he'd set aside his Bible and begun to pray, thanking God for always being there, even when Richard had gotten too busy and neglected the relationship he shared with his Heavenly Father.

When Angela had knocked on the door, he had realized he hadn't had lunch and it was nearing dinnertime.

He was hungry.

"Why don't you sit over here?" Angela offered, pointing to one of the empty chairs at the small table. Before he could thank her, she scurried away, heading toward the living room.

The dining room area had a thin rug tossed over old wooden floorboards. An ancient-looking hutch and warming board sat to one side, while on the other side of the table was a chest. Beyond that was the kitchen, and in the opposite direction was the communal living room where Angela had disappeared.

Spaghetti and garlic bread sat on the table. He couldn't remember the last time he'd had such a simple but delicious-looking meal.

Richard made his way over to the sturdy wooden chair and lowered himself into it. Leaning his crutches against the wall behind him, he settled in.

Or so he thought. Just as he finished adjusting his leg he saw Angela return, with Granny. With dawning realization, he saw the only place available for her to sit was at the end of the table, directly to his right. Subconsciously, he rubbed his left leg, glad it was protected. However, even though he was worried about the woman and some possible unforeseen antics she might decide to play, he smiled politely as Granny was positioned at the head of the table.

Angela came around the six-seater table and grabbed a chair next to him. Samantha brought napkins to finish off the table and took the seat opposite Richard's and on Granny's other side.

Nodding to Granny he said politely, "Hello."

"You," the woman said clearly, and thumped the table.

Surprised, he leaned back slightly.

"Granny!" Samantha said, embarrassed, if the way her cheeks heated up with a pink tint was an indication. Turning to Richard, she continued, "There are a few words that Granny says clearly. There are even some she can write down. She's well able to make her point in most cases."

Turning back to Granny, she said, "This is our renter, remember? He's our guest."

Granny scowled at him.

Angela grinned.

Richard could only wonder why Granny had taken an instant dislike to him and why Angela found that amusing.

"We usually pray before our meals," Samantha said.

Richard realized Samantha was telling him, and he replied, "I think that is a very refreshing idea." He bowed his head.

As Samantha spoke, her sweet gentle voice washed over him. She talked with God as one would a Father, openly and honestly and in simple terms. There were no put-ons here, no fancy words or blessings called down. She mentioned that she had enjoyed the cold weather and snow, and was so very happy to have a new boarder, and then thanked Him for all of the great blessings He had given her. Then she mentioned Richard's ankle and asked God to hurry along the healing. She finally thanked Him for giving her such wonderful people to share a meal with and then closed the prayer.

Richard couldn't describe how her prayer for his ankle had touched him.

Something inside him warmed.

"So," Samantha said, interrupting his thoughts, "I hope you like spaghetti."

She passed the bowl of noodles to him. "It's been too long since I had it," he replied gently, smiling at Samantha.

She wore jeans and a white top that was stained with chocolate. Small tendrils of damp hair hung around her face, and she looked like she'd just finished cooking.

But she was still beautiful.

"Sam thought with you new here and all, you wouldn't have had time to go shopping or even feel like cooking." This was put in by Angela.

Finished with the noodles, he handed them to Angela, who placed them back in the middle of the table.

"That is certainly true," Richard replied, wishing it were only he and Samantha at the table. Ah well, so much for romance—with a glaring Granny and an inquisitive Angela.

Samantha had placed some Italian sausage and noodles on Granny's plate and cut it up. She helped Granny grab the spoon and then turned back to her own plate and began to fill it.

"How are you feeling?" Samantha asked, concern in her voice.

"Do I look that bad?" Richard quipped. He accepted a piece of garlic bread and nodded his thanks to Angela.

"I'd say so," Angela teased.

"Nice kid," Richard murmured.

She grinned cheekily. "You gotta love me. My dad says so—all the time."

After a heartbeat of astonishment at this young woman's comeback, he burst into laughter. "Then, you must have a great dad."

"I sure do," she replied, and dipped her fork into the spaghetti on her plate.

"To answer your question," Richard said, returning his gaze to Samantha, "I am a bit tired. Getting used to the strain of crutches is going to take a day or two. I fear Dillon will be making quite a few trips for me to the store until some of these unknown muscles toughen up."

"I was afraid of that," Samantha said. She glanced over at her grandmother, who slowly managed to scoop some food onto her spoon and lift it to her mouth.

"I take it from that comment that you've had crutches before?"

Samantha chuckled. "Oh yes. If Granny could tell you all the times she took me to the emergency room." Swirling her fork, she caught up some more spaghetti and took a bite.

"Fortunately, I rarely go to the doctor. However, the ER doctor said this was minor."

"My uncle is a good doctor," Angela piped up as she reached for a second piece of garlic bread.

For one so small she had quite an appetite—and mouth, Richard thought. For some reason, though, he found himself liking the sprite. "An uncle?"

"Or my aunt."

"Ah. Both are doctors?"

She nodded.

"Julian, and Susan, aka Freckles McCade," Samantha put in patiently.

"Well, actually, her name isn't Freckles but that's what everyone calls her. They have a clinic just outside of town. Uncle Julian was going to leave town as soon as he finished up his time served out at the clinic. That was before. Now he's staying and he and his wife are working full time out there. They're planning to hire two more doctors soon, just so they can keep their practice they've opened in town going as well.''

Boy, did she have a lot of information stored in here. He'd remember not to tell her a secret.

''It must be nice having a doctor in the family,'' Richard replied politely.

''And the sheriff.''

''Pardon me?'' Richard glanced to Samantha for clarification.

Samantha smiled. ''Her other uncle is the sheriff of Hill Creek. And her dad is a rancher.''

''Very different jobs.''

''They all felt they had different callings in their lives,'' Samantha said.

''Most sons follow in their dad's footsteps,'' Richard replied matter-of-factly.

''Dad did,'' Angela replied.

Samantha added, ''I grew up with Zach—her dad—and Mitch, though Julian was a bit younger than me. When their parents died, it was Zach's sheer determination that kept them together. He was plunged into the ranching business full time. I think, for a while, that the brothers were lost. It takes its toll, losing your father so young.''

Richard tilted his head. ''It sounds as if you speak from experience.''

"I lost my dad much younger, actually. The McCades were teenagers. I was seven."

"I'm sorry," Richard replied.

Samantha shrugged. "Don't be. I had Granny."

He wanted to ask about her mother. That was twice now she'd referred to Granny as if she was the one who had raised Samantha. "My dad is still alive, as is my grandfather and grandmother. My mother, however, died when I was quite young."

Surprisingly, Samantha said, "My mother died several years ago, but really, I lost her the day my dad left." She smiled over at her grandmother. "But then, I've always had Granny."

That explained a lot. Richard wasn't sure what to say in response to her revelation. She was so open and honest about everything, it boggled the mind. He had told Samantha some facts, but hadn't admitted that his father was a very driven man and that he had got the nurturing from his grandda. Yet, she'd laid out the details without blinking, as if he were an old friend who had the right to know.

His heart swelled at her trust. "Then, Granny must be very special." He smiled at Granny.

She scowled at him and slammed her spoon down. "Um dun..."

He blinked.

"Cantankerous in her old age," Samantha said, gazing fondly at Granny.

Granny grinned back and cackled.

Samantha removed the plate and helped Granny clean up. "I love her, though. And you're right, she is very, very special."

Granny looked lovingly at her granddaughter. "Un ah auv ooh."

"I'll be right back. I need to take Granny into the living room."

"I'm actually done, if you are," Richard said, noting Samantha's empty plate.

"Then, won't you join us in the living room?"

He nodded.

"Don't worry about me. I'll just clear these dishes," Angela said.

Richard turned to see Angela's grin and asked, "Would you like some help?"

"You'd break your other leg trying to maneuver with dishes."

"It's Angela's job in the house to clear the dishes, Richard. Don't let her fool you."

Angela giggled as if she'd pulled a fast one and stood. She started clearing the table.

Richard grabbed his crutches and slowly stood. "You've got your hands full with her."

He followed Samantha into the other room.

"She gets a break on the apartment by doing dishes. Of course, I have a dishwasher, but when she moved in, she admitted to hating to cook, so I struck a deal. If she eats with me, she clears the table and loads the dishwasher. She gets out of buying groceries and cooking, though she does occasionally cook just to give me a break."

"She seems like a nice kid."

"She's almost twenty-three. Which means she's a kid no longer."

Richard nodded. "I remember those days. And the things I did. I definitely wasn't a kid at that age."

The cozy living room had that nice lived-in look. On the coffee table and side tables were magazines and the occasional book. CDs were piled up on a player and a TV sat on a small cherry-wood table in the corner.

The fireplace burned, giving off the woodsy smell of ash. It added warmth to what otherwise would have been a chilly room.

"Granny likes fires, so in the winter I try to keep one going."

She parked Granny's chair next to one of the wing chairs. Granny reached for the *Reader's Digest* on the table and plunked it on the built-in tray atop her wheelchair.

She obviously was settled in for the night and was going to ignore them all.

Samantha went to the fireplace to toss another log onto the fire. In the area next to the fireplace stood a three-foot-high stack of wood.

Placing the screen back in place, Samantha returned and seated herself next to Granny. Richard took the sofa and propped his foot up on the coffee table.

"I'm sorry you had to miss the New Year's celebration at church," Samantha said.

In the kitchen they could hear dishes being loaded. Granny was engrossed in the book before her. It felt like the two of them were alone in the quiet living room, the crackling fire their only company.

"Don't worry about it. It was an impulse to go there."

Samantha frowned. "You don't go to church?"

Richard sighed. Leaning his head back against

the top of the sofa, he admitted, "Over the past few years it seems I've gotten out of the habit of attending regularly." He hesitated, but the darkened room, the fire seemed to provide an intimacy between them that made him want to confess things he might never admit to anyone else. "I had gotten so involved in life and work that somewhere along the way, God took second place."

Samantha didn't comment. As the quiet lengthened, he added, "Something happened recently that made me realize things weren't right. I've slowly begun a journey of discovery, you could say. I've been working my way back to things lost. And I finally realized that one of the reasons things were so out of kilter in my life was that I'd lost that first love I had, for God."

"Oh dear," Samantha murmured.

Richard rolled his head to the side where he rested it back on the sofa. "Not to worry. That was my first step. Just because I never made it in the church door doesn't mean my mind has been changed. I spent a wonderful time today reading my Bible and getting reacquainted with God."

Frowning, Samantha nodded. "I think it should be my responsibility while your ankle is out of commission to see that you get to church."

Surprised, Richard responded, "That's not necessary."

"But I insist. It's my fault your ankle was broken in the first place."

"You'd be better off not to argue with her," Angela piped in from the doorway.

Richard's head turned. Angela wasn't alone.

A tall, young man, most likely part Mexican, stood next to her along with another young woman. He thought at first it might be a boyfriend of Angela's, but there was something familiar about the way she stood by him.

Ah…he carried a doctor's bag.

"Julian!" Samantha said. "What are you doing here?"

Julian McCade smiled and came into the room. "I'm running late today, Samantha. Freckles had some patients she needed help with, so I didn't make it by this afternoon. Your home-health nurse should have mentioned that to you. At any rate, I'm here to check out Granny now. You know my sister-in-law, Sherrie? She's acting as a nursing assistant to me and goes on my house calls. She's decided she wants to be a nurse." He beamed at the young girl at his side.

No more than seventeen, the girl had her dark

hair pinned back on her head and wore a set of scrubs similar to Julian's. While Julian's were dark blue and solid, the girl's top had a pink floral design.

"Angela, will you take Granny to her room so they can examine her?" Samantha asked.

Granny scowled at Richard, then thumped her chair. Dr. McCade evidently wasn't used to such actions from Granny. His gaze went from Granny to Richard and back.

"This is my new renter. He's also looking for a doctor. If you have time, stop back by on your way out and I'll tell you the story," Samantha said.

Julian offered a warm smile. "I'll do that, Sam." He turned to Richard. "We'll be back in a few minutes."

Angela gathered up Granny and together they left the room.

"I don't suppose it ever slows down here?" Richard asked wryly.

Samantha chuckled. "You're kidding. Just wait until we start our February push. Angela and I will be putting in long nights." Samantha's smile faded. "I hate to see Angie work so hard. She's in vet school and I am worried her studies are going to suffer.''

Richard frowned. "Kids are resilient. My last year of college I worked full time as well as attending school. It was hard, I'll admit, but some of us just thrive on that.''

''I wouldn't know.''

''You didn't work when you went to college?'' Richard asked.

''I didn't go to college,'' Samantha replied.

''Ah.'' Richard was afraid he'd made a faux pas, but Samantha waved her hand.

''My grandmother had a stroke fifteen years ago. My mother was an alcoholic from the time my father left—probably before. You know how kids don't necessarily notice those things. I think Dad might have known. Anyway, so I started helping Granny. I was seventeen when she had her first stroke and I had to start running the store. Five years ago, when I turned twenty-seven, my mom died and I was officially the one in charge.''

''So you really know what you're talking about when you say that Angela isn't necessarily a kid.''

Samantha chuckled. "Oh yeah. Some kids have such drive that at a young age they can accomplish many things. Angela has that drive, though she does still have a childish side as well.''

"And you don't," Richard said softly.

Her smile faded a bit. "I haven't had time. But I don't regret it. I wish sometimes that Granny was better and could walk again. She gets physical and occupational therapy and is slowly learning to talk. She's had three more minor strokes since the big one. The last one put her in a wheelchair. Julian says she'll probably get out of it, eventually. At least, we hope she does. And she is talking again. Somewhat.'' Samantha sighed.

Richard's heart felt like it was going to explode in his chest. He couldn't believe the love this woman had inside her. And yet, who was there to love her?

She took care of Granny. She'd taken Angela in and, though Angela was an employee, it sounded like Samantha treated her like a younger sister. And now she was caring for him.

He had never been one to believe in love at first sight. But maybe, love in the first twenty-four hours?

It sounded so sappy, like those crazy commercials he thought up when he was working that department several years ago in the business.

At thirty-six, Richard did not really believe in that silly kind of love. Love was a relationship that developed over time, where two people had the same likes and dislikes or the same goals for the future.

But now, tonight, sitting here in the flickering firelight, Richard thought that attraction—the need to hold and care for this woman despite the fact that they were from two different worlds— and that feeling inside him, the one that said this was the woman for him, was more important than anything else.

Richard struggled up and, taking his crutches, hobbled over to the fire. "Have you seen your dad recently? Is he still alive?"

Samantha stiffened, her smile freezing.

That fast, he'd broken the mood.

"I don't want him in my life."

"Ah," Richard said.

"He does carpentry work on buildings. I've heard he comes to town occasionally, and about once a year or sometimes more often he stops by to say hi, but we don't have anything to say to each other." She shrugged.

In that shrug was a wealth of meaning.

Samantha had never recovered from the loss of her dad.

She had walked up next to him and now studied the fire. He turned slightly and touched her shoulder. Then, when she glanced at him, he nodded to the sofa.

She moved there with him.

As they sat down, her shoulder brushed his. The sweet fresh smell of cinnamon drifted up from Samantha and he wanted to curl his hand in her hair and sniff it again.

Instead, he satisfied himself with reaching up and stroking her hair back behind one of her ears.

Samantha's eyes widened.

He smiled gently. "Have I told you how upside down you've turned me in just twenty-four hours?"

She swallowed and shook her head.

He nodded. "Meeting you has thrown my entire world into—"

"A mess?" she asked.

He chuckled and stroked her cheek before backing off. "Let's just say that I haven't felt this relaxed since I don't know when."

He thought about it and tried to remember the last time he'd enjoyed a woman's presence.

It was hard, since they all knew who he was and...

His warm feelings came to a sudden halt as he realized that, though he was falling hard and fast for this woman, there was something that blocked him from going further.

She didn't know who he was.

Samantha sat there smiling at him, the fire in the background highlighting the golden tones of her hair, and all he could think of was that if she found out who he was...

He had to tell her.

*Now.*

His emotions were doing things they had never done before, he was feeling things he had never felt before. This was crazy!

Better to get everything out in the open and then they would be on even ground. After all, if what he thought he might be feeling was real, then he had to confess everything.

''Samantha—''

''Granny looks fine. Now, what's up with your guest?'' Julian and his assistant came back into the room.

Richard nearly groaned out loud at their imperfect timing.

"It's a long story," Samantha admitted.

That fast, the opportunity to tell her who he was had passed.

With a sigh he put on a polite face and turned to Dr. McCade. "It seems I have a hairline fracture," he admitted.

"So, why don't you tell me how it happened?" Julian said, and took a nearby chair.

Thus, the tone for the night had been set.

# Chapter Seven

*She was dancing. It was her wedding.*

*Samantha was so very happy. Wearing a beautifully crafted white lace wedding gown with an empire waist and long, lacy sleeves, she held on to the man in front of her as they swung around and around, waltzing to the music.*

*The trail of her gown flowed out a good four feet and she felt as if she danced on air. The joy and excitement she felt as this man held her was indescribable.*

*She looked up into Richard's eyes and knew she had finally come home, until—*

*Her grandmother wheeled over and, with the*

*strength of a bull, shoved between the two of them, breaking them up.*

*Samantha stumbled back.*

*Granny hit the man over and over, saying, "done...rush...done"—what she'd been saying since he'd first come into their house, when she'd had her therapy, when she'd sat reading her magazines, when she'd watched TV. Samantha would be there, usually alone with her and suddenly Granny would pop up with her new word* done. *But why? Why did she want it over with this man?*

*Suddenly Richard nodded. "I am done. I am in a rush. I have to go." Sadly he looked at Samantha and said, "I'm sorry...."*

*Without moving his feet, he started backing away and, as he did, his body got smaller and smaller.*

*"No!" she cried out, reaching for him. He cared for her, he warmed her heart the way no other man had. She didn't want him to go.*

*"No! No!"*

With a gasp, she sat up.

Blinking, she glanced around the room.

She'd been asleep, dreaming. About her boarder!

Something had awakened her.

"Come on, Samantha! Get up! You're running late!"

Angela pounded on her door.

Looking to the clock, she groaned. It was almost 9:00 a.m. "I'm coming!" Samantha called out. "I'll be right there. Go open without me, please."

She was thankful that Angela didn't return to school for another week. She would have been late opening today if Angela had already left.

And Granny!

Leaping from bed, she rushed toward the shower. The home-health nurse was already here doing therapy. Samantha usually showed up for that. But she hadn't this morning.

Samantha could smell that someone had fixed breakfast. Oh dear. Angela must have cooked for Granny. She had a cook that came in and fixed breakfast and lunch because she was too busy to cook. They always had a nice fresh breakfast and a cold lunch. But the cook was off for two more days.

Jumping in the shower, she didn't wait for it to warm up, but simply suffered through the cold. In minutes she was out and pulling on her pants and top. Four days now. He had been in her house four days and her sleeping patterns were a mess. She dreamed of him every night. She watched for glimpses of him when the man came to install the phone line, when his friend Dillon came by, and felt elated when he came down for supper.

And each night they'd gotten to know each other a little better. It'd be a lot better if not for Angela and Granny.

She felt guilty for that last thought.

Running a quick brush through her hair, allowing only the merest amount of time to apply makeup, she checked her reflection and then rushed down the stairs.

For once in her life she really wished she had time free to spend with a man.

The bell over the door jangled as she entered the kitchen, so Samantha made a detour to the front of the store.

She heard the voice before she saw him. "Well, hello there, darlin'"

It was Liam Slater. And it wasn't *that* man she was thinking about when she wanted time alone.

"Oh, it's you," Angela's tart voice replied.

*Oh dear.* Angela was a pretty good worker, except when it came to this man.

"I was on my way to the bank, but thought I'd

stop in and place an order. I need a box of chocolates for a date tonight.''

''You and your dates.''

This was building into another one of Angela's cut-downs. Rushing in, Samantha stopped just short and smoothed the yellow top she wore. ''Good morning, Liam. Did I hear you ask for a box of chocolates?''

Liam was easily six feet two inches tall and had dark hair and eyes. He was as handsome as they come—to most women. He'd never interested Samantha, being two years behind her in school and not being a Christian. He was also known as one of the wild boys of Hill Creek.

Lately, however, he'd had his eye on Angela.

Liam turned that megawatt smile on her. ''I sure do, honey. I've got me another date tonight.''

Samantha smiled politely. ''When do you not have a date, Liam?''

He chuckled. ''It's a shame you're a Christian.''

She shook her head at his statement. Angela started fixing up the normal twelve-item candy box that he always wanted, so Samantha turned her attention fully on Liam. ''Some would disagree.''

Liam's smile faltered slightly.

"How's Drake?"

His smile returned. "My brother is doing well. He had to go into the wheelchair for a while last week. The winters seem harder on him than other times. But he's back out of it now."

His brother had been trampled by a bull a few years back and nearly lost his life. To hear him tell it, the only thing that saved him was an Angel of the Lord that he saw stopping the bull just short of killing him. That was why he gave his life to God, right there on the spot, finally realizing that God was real. That's what he told anyone who would listen. He was so in love with God and his newfound relationship. If things hadn't been bad enough, on the operating table he'd had a stroke. No one had expected him to live, but then, that just went to show Samantha that when God was in control, He could perform miracles.

"And Tessa?" Drake had married the local schoolteacher who'd taken on teaching him to read again during the summer of his recovery.

"She's expecting number three any day now."

Samantha smiled. "Give them my love."

"I'd rather have it," Liam said, and placed a hand over his heart.

Samantha rolled her eyes. "You big flirt."

Angela slapped the pale blue box up on the counter, drawing both of their gazes. "Here you go."

"Since she won't give me hers," he said, referring to Angela.

Angela scowled.

Liam pulled out the money and laid it on the counter. Winking at Angela, he said, "Thanks, darlin'." And, scooping up the box, he headed out the door, whistling.

"I hate that man," Angela said, glaring at his back.

Samantha turned slightly to study her employee. "*Hate* is such a strong word."

"Oh, you know what I mean." She sighed. "He acts so sure of himself, so in charge, but anytime anyone mentions Christianity he treats it with contempt, or worse, laughs it off."

Samantha wasn't sure what to say. "Perhaps. You do know he went through a hard time when his parents died, and then he almost lost his brother. Some people don't understand God's ways."

"Who's that?" Richard asked, coming into the store.

There was the man she wanted to spend time with—no comparison to the one who'd just left. Samantha caught her breath. Richard was dressed in dark pants, a dress shirt and that tweed jacket again. He was devastatingly handsome, she realized, even with the crutches.

"Some guy that comes in here all the time buying candies for his many dates."

Richard lifted his eyebrows and a small smile touched his lips. Samantha wondered what he was thinking.

"Look at it this way, Angie," Samantha said, straightening the counter before going to the small tables and starting to lay out the napkin containers. "At least he isn't a liar."

"Well, that's true."

"I mean, he could be a fake and pretend to be a Christian or put on airs or constantly lie to you. Though Liam isn't a Christian, he doesn't lie about the fact. He also is very honest about who he is and what he does. Personally, I think he's searching. When people run from God, they do things that they normally wouldn't do. With Liam, my guess is that he's still hurting and that's why you see him with so many different women. If we keep praying for him, he'll come around."

"I suppose."

The bell sounded again. Samantha glanced up just in time to see Zach McCade enter the store. "Dad!"

Inwardly, Samantha sighed. So much for having a moment to talk to Richard.

Angela grinned and scooted around the counter to hug her dad. In tow was her five-year-old half sister. She gave her a hug, as well.

"I came by to see if you could join us for breakfast."

"I already ate but…"

Angela looked at Samantha. Samantha was running behind on fixing some of her specialty candy and really needed Angela here, but Angela had such a close relationship with her dad, there was no way she'd ask Angela to miss out on a date with him. "Go ahead."

"Let me get my purse."

She dashed off.

Richard moved forward.

"So you're the man Sam ran down?" Zach asked.

Samantha looked over at Richard and flushed. Turning a glare on one of her childhood tormentors, whom she now thought of as a friend, she said, "Very funny, Zach. This is Richard."

Richard stuck his hand out, over the counter, and Zach reached over and shook it. "You've got a sweet daughter," Richard commented.

"Daddy, can we have candy?" asked the little girl next to her dad. With her long blond hair and beautiful blue eyes, she looked up beguilingly.

"After breakfast we'll stop back by and get some."

Her lower lip stuck out. Zach rubbed her head. Just then, Angela returned. "Come on, Angie-doll before my other doll here throws a fit."

Samantha laughed.

"Nice meeting you," Zach said, and ambled out with Samantha's help.

The shop quieted.

On second thought, Samantha might just get some time with Richard. Tentatively, she turned back to him. "Well, quiet again."

"He looks like a hard worker," Richard commented.

"He is. He owns a ranch just outside of town. His wife, Laura, works for Mitch, the sheriff."

"Dispatcher?"

Samantha shook her head. "Deputy."

"I'll be glad to help you until Angela gets back."

Surprised, Samantha asked, "What do you know about waiting on people?"

Richard chuckled. "Not a lot. But I can finish putting out the napkin holders, stoke up the fire, get anything you need from the supply room, things like that."

"On crutches?" Samantha asked doubtfully.

He nodded. Swinging his legs, he said, "I think I'm getting the hang of it."

As if to prove him wrong, his left crutch hit a slick spot on the floor and flew out from under him.

Richard teetered.

Samantha gasped and jumped forward.

Richard fell into Samantha.

This time, however, Samantha was standing on a padded rubber mat. Because of that, she had leverage and didn't stagger and fall as his body fell into hers. Turning slightly, she allowed her back to come up against the tall counter.

Richard's arm went around Samantha as he tried to protect her and regain his balance.

He steadied himself quickly. However, his arm stayed around her as he pushed back enough to

look down at her face. "No, I don't think you can
help," she tried to joke, lifting her gaze to his.

*Zap.*

There it was again—that electricity between
them.

"Samantha," Richard said quietly.

Samantha's hands ran up the front of his tweed
jacket. The musky smell of cologne mixed with
soap and him actually sparked longing within her.

She couldn't have torn her gaze away from him
if her life depended on it.

Richard lowered his head and his lips touched
hers.

Just like in the dream, Samantha thought, and
returned the kiss.

It felt so right.

His warmth surrounded her, protected her and
actually made her feel as if she could lean on him
for support. How long had it been since she felt
protected and cared for?

From the moment she saw this man, she'd been
attracted to him.

Her mind screamed out that this was silly. She
had Granny to care for, a store that was going
under and a million and one other things to worry
about.

But this man, right now, felt so right.

Suddenly, he was gone. Stepping back, he winced.

"Oh dear!" Samantha said, remembering his ankle. She scrambled over to where the crutch had fallen, grabbed it and held it out to Richard.

Needless to say, she felt her cheeks turning red. "I'm sorry," she offered.

He adjusted his crutches, then said, "Don't be." Finally, he lifted his eyes to hers. "I normally don't kiss a woman before I've at least taken her out on a couple of dates."

Samantha turned even redder.

"It's okay," Richard said. "Really. Unless you objected?" he added.

"Did it look or feel like I objected?" Samantha asked, flabbergasted by her own reaction. Embarrassed, she turned and finished putting out the napkin holders, then started stacking new gift boxes by size and color.

What had gotten into her? She didn't have time for this. Of course, Granny had always said when love hit her, it'd hit her hard and all at once.

But this wasn't love.

It couldn't be.

"Samantha."

His voice sent good shivers tingling throughout her. "Sometimes love just happens."

"Love? I don't— I— Love? We've only just met each other." She waved a hand in the air. "Attraction? Yes. I mean, we haven't gone out on a date or anything. How can it be—"

"Then, go out with me tonight."

Samantha's heart pounded. Turning, she looked up at Richard. "Tonight?"

He smiled. "If you drive."

She glanced down at his ankle and felt immediately guilty. "Okay."

He frowned. "That had better be because you want to go and not because you feel guilty."

Samantha hesitated. "If Sherrie can sit with Granny tonight, it's the least I can do."

Richard swung forward, taking each step carefully, watching for any more slick spots on the cement floor. He stopped just in front of her. "I want you to go out because of the attraction we feel."

She swallowed.

"If you don't feel it, then I'll back off right now. It'd be nice to have someone to talk with, share dinner, tell her what's been going on in my life since arriving in Hill Creek, or maybe even before.'' His warm, spine-tingling smile returned and in a low deep voice, he added, ''It'd also be nice simply to enjoy looking across the table at such a lovely woman.''

Oh! Samantha felt herself drowning, going down for the third time. Richard's charm was lethal and she hadn't had her immunity shot. ''I—''

''Please?''

Any reserve she had melted away. ''Okay.''

He reached up with one hand and cupped her cheek. ''Thank you, Samantha.''

The door jingled again.

''Did I come at a bad time?''

Both turned to see Dillon standing there.

Richard dropped his hand.

''Or perhaps just in time,'' Dillon added.

Samantha didn't understand what he meant, but evidently Richard did, if the odd look on his face was an indicator.

''I hate to interrupt, Richard, but can we go out for breakfast?'' Dillon asked.

Richard turned toward Dillon, working his way around the counter. ''Okay. Just...'' His voice trailed off.

He paused and glanced back at Samantha. ''Are you sure you don't need my help?''

She appeared skeptical about how much help he could truly be in his state. She nodded.

"Until tonight," he said, and headed out the door with Dillon.

Left standing there, embarrassingly enough, all she could think about was that she couldn't wait for tonight.

# Chapter Eight

"I thought you might enjoy some company."

Richard stood in the living room doorway of Samantha's house. The TV was on with a black-and-white movie playing and Granny sat watching it. He was dressed and ready for dinner, though there was still a half hour before he was supposed to meet Samantha for their date.

At his words, Granny swiveled her head toward him and scowled.

He slowly entered the room and carefully took a seat next to her—not too close. He didn't want to give her a chance to pull at his pants again.

Peculiar woman.

Was she always so unhappy? he wondered. He shifted and set his crutches aside.

"Uhh," the woman grunted.

"Your granddaughter rented out an upstairs apartment to me and so it'd be nice if we got to know each other," he said.

The woman lifted a hand and waved it in the air.

Richard nodded. Turning his attention to the TV, he watched for a few minutes before realizing what show this was. "*Shop Around the Corner.* I saw that aeons ago with my grandda. It's about a woman who owns a store and this man who comes…" His voice trailed off as he realized it was very similar to what was going on in his own life at the moment.

A magazine hit him on the side of the head.

He jumped. Turning incredulous eyes toward the old woman, he asked, "Did you not like the magazine?"

She glared at him and pointed.

He picked it up and turned it over. He saw nothing that warranted such behavior. It was simply a chatty magazine that talked about different celebrities and what went on in their lives. He knew of it because his company took out a lot of ads in the magazine.

"Look," he said, frustration growing as he set the magazine aside. "I can certainly say I am not sure what I've done, but possibly I've offended you in some way. Perhaps we should start over."

The woman was once again watching the show, pretending he wasn't there.

He sighed. Maybe this wasn't such a good idea. He couldn't communicate with her, after all.

He turned to see what was being played out on the telly and simply sat in silence. Then he picked up the magazine and started flipping through it…until he saw the advertisement. Surely the old woman hadn't recognized the picture of him as a child in the Dunnington's ad!

He glanced sideways at her with a curious look. She was glaring at him again.

Oh-oh, he thought.

With a sigh he set the magazine aside. No wonder she'd bopped him on the head with it.

Finally, he said softly, "I love her, you know."

Shifting, he straightened out his injured leg. His gaze wandered to where Samantha had sat last night, where the firelight had played off her beautiful hair. "I know it sounds crazy. I don't even know why I'm telling you. I came in here hoping to win your approval. You see, you're right, I'm not who she thinks and I'm going to try to correct that mistake tonight.''

He had the woman's attention now.

''Done,'' she said, the garbled noise not making much sense.

He nodded, but he knew by the look on the woman's face that she had realized he didn't know what she meant. ''I'm sorry. I suppose it's very frustrating being in a body that won't allow you to communicate what you're thinking.'' Maybe she meant she was glad he had done what she wanted?

Granny nodded and thumped the top of her chair.

''I don't want to hurt your granddaughter. From what I've heard, she's already had plenty of that.''

Granny reached in a bag attached to the side of her wheelchair and pulled out a puzzle book.

She tried to pick up a pen that was anchored by a string to the top of her chair.

Richard watched for only a minute before he realized she wasn't going to be able to get it into her good hand without help. Shoving himself up, he hopped over to her side. He leaned down, caught the pen in his fingers and helped her anchor it in her hand.

She grabbed at his pants leg again and pulled.

He glanced at her and she pointed at the magazine.

"You are very observant. Yes, that was me as a child. In the kilt. I was very young at the time and I like to think that I can't be recognized as that boy."

She grinned and cackled.

Relief melted him.

He returned his attention to helping her hold the writing instrument in her crippled hand.

She hesitated and then looked up at him and nodded.

As she did, he noticed tears in her eyes.

Something inside him moved as he realized this woman really was smart as a whip, as Angela had said. Maybe her anger at him stemmed partly from the fact that she was angry at her situation. Or perhaps it was that she saw the attraction he held for her granddaughter and she was afraid she might lose her. Or perhaps it was that he hadn't told her granddaughter the truth.

Granny returned to the find-a-word and with

her crippled hand shoved at the pages until she found an empty one. Holding the book in place with the left limb, she placed the pen on the right-hand side and started studying the pages.

Richard hopped back over to his seat.

"Oh!"

Richard glanced around to see that Samantha had pulled up short in the doorway. In her right arm she carried a Bible while both hands held a tray.

"I didn't know you were down here. I brought Granny a bedtime snack. Cookies and milk."

Richard smiled. When she entered the room, everything else faded. The impact this woman had would shake a lesser man, he thought. It was scary for him to realize how vulnerable he felt when she was around.

He, the world traveler who rubbed elbows with the most sophisticated women in society, was suddenly defenseless with this woman. His grandda would laugh.

"I usually read to her right now, but I can wait."

Richard shook his head. "Go ahead. What are you reading?"

She held up the book. "The Bible."

Wryly, he grinned.

She answered with a silly smile.

"I meant, what in the Bible are you reading?"

"Oh!" The way her cheeks changed to such a light shade of pink enchanted him. "We're starting First John today."

He nodded. "Do you mind if I stay and listen?"

She smiled. "Not at all."

Turning the sound down on the TV, Samantha then came over and sat down next to Granny.

Granny smiled a sweet, loving smile and reached out to touch her granddaughter's hair with her left hand, the hand that was partially crippled. Richard found himself wishing he were included in that moment as more than a simple observer.

Samantha smiled back into Granny's eyes.

They had a very special relationship, he thought, watching them. He remembered his grandmother and the same touches from her when he was a little boy.

No wonder Granny had been so contrary with him. But tonight would solve that. Later. Now he was simply going to enjoy Samantha's presence.

Samantha turned and began to read. She read

while she helped Granny eat the snack and then continued to read after Granny had finished eating.

She read the entire book of First John.

When Samantha was done, Granny looked like she was drooping with exhaustion. As if on cue, the part-time nurse walked in. "Time for bed."

With the smile that every nurse wore, the one that said, *I care and everything is perfect in the world today,* she walked across the room and grabbed the back of the wheelchair.

Samantha stood, leaned down and kissed Granny on the cheek and then stepped back out of the way.

They both watched the nurse take her out.

"So, are you headed back to work?" Richard asked.

Samantha shook her head. "I have two part-time girls in there who are closing up for me. I should start to work on the candy, but frankly, this entire day has been off kilter and we're going out, so it's just going to have to wait."

"I can leave if you need some time to yourself," Richard offered, and reached for his crutches.

"No! Stay."

Surprised, he glanced over at her. The pink hue had deepened, and in her eyes, he saw a yearning. For his company.

He nodded. "I'd be delighted."

A look of relief crossed her face and she sat down.

She grabbed the remote control. "This was one of my favorite movies. Granny and I used to watch it whenever it came on—usually every winter." She pointed the remote and turned the TV off. "Granny had a good day."

"It looked like it," Richard agreed. "She really loves you."

Samantha nodded. "And I love her. I guess you've figured out she basically raised me."

Richard shrugged, knowing from what Samantha had told him yesterday that it was redundant to repeat it. Instead, he said, "I want to thank you for renting out the apartment to me."

"It's my fault your ankle is broken."

Richard shook his head. "Don't, Sam. Stop taking responsibility for everything."

"But—"

He interrupted her. "If you hadn't run me down, we wouldn't have met."

Her mouth formed a small *O* as she digested what he'd said.

Finally, she admitted, "I'm glad we met."

"So am I," he murmured.

"Well then," she said. Standing, she brushed her hands down the gray wool slacks she wore. "Are you ready to go?"

He nodded and stood. Grabbing up his crutches, he placed them under his arms. "The doctor wants me to come in Monday. He said they might put a walking cast on my foot." After coming home from breakfast with Dillon, Richard had been busy. Not only had he had a conference call with his father and grandda, he'd been in touch with several people back in New York pertaining to business. He'd actually fallen asleep for a short time. When he'd awakened, he'd called Dr. McCade and set up an appointment. Though McCade wasn't an orthopedist, Richard was impressed with the man and thought he would prefer going to him.

"That's great. Is Dillon going to drive you?"

Richard nodded. "And then, hopefully, I'll be driving myself after that."

They went to the front of the living room and exited the house through a side door that led them around to her truck. He stopped by the driver's side, and when she pulled her keys out, he reached for them.

"You can't drive!" Samantha said, alarm ringing in her voice.

He turned the lock and opened the door. Handing the keys back to her, he smiled. "I know."

It only took a moment for her to realize he was being a gentleman. Her eyes turned liquid. "I don't think anyone has ever opened my door for me."

Stunned, Richard allowed a laugh of disbelief to escape. "You cannot be serious."

Slowly, she nodded.

He reached out and touched her chin. "Then, you've been dating the wrong men, my dear."

She swallowed.

Forcing her gaze away from his gentle caring one, she got into the truck.

Richard moved around the vehicle and paused to toss his crutches in the bed. He carefully eased himself into the tiny cab and then closed his own door, which she had reached across and unlocked for him before starting the engine.

"There's a nice restaurant in the mall I'd like to go to, if you don't mind."

"The Mexican one?" she asked.

He'd had Dillon scope out the good restaurants for him today and it looked like, unless they left Hill Creek, the Mexican restaurant was the best. "That's the one," he affirmed.

She backed up and turned onto the sand-covered street.

"It's stopped snowing," Samantha observed.

"But the wind chill is still very much present," Richard countered.

"We have a lot of wind out here."

He nodded. "So does Southern California."

"You've been to California?" Samantha asked as they drove the two blocks to the mall.

He nodded. "I sure have. And Lincoln, Nebraska, where it's windy as well."

"You travel a lot."

He nodded.

As they started to turn into the mall, he noticed a flower shop across the street. "Wait. Turn there," he said, pointing to a parking place just down from the shop.

Samantha did as he asked. "That's a long way to walk."

He only grinned. "Stay here."

He shoved open the door and reached for his crutches.

Samantha watched him go. When she realized where he was heading, she gasped. It had been a wild, hectic day. She'd only seen Richard leave this morning and hadn't known when he returned. He'd been on her mind all day. The shop had seemed empty and not right with him away, and she'd made so many mistakes because she'd been unable to keep her mind on the business.

She couldn't believe what she felt for this man. He'd blindsided her. And she didn't know what to do about it.

Richard came back out with a small bouquet of red flowers.

Tears burned her eyes.

He tossed his crutches in the back, opened the door and leaned in. "These go well with the red top you have on," he said.

"Thank you," she whispered, taking them.

He struggled in and closed the door. Holding his hands in front of the heater, he said, "You don't seem pleased."

She shrugged. "These are the first flowers I've received."

"My," Richard said, so properly that she

nearly laughed. "Are all of the men here blind and totally without any sense?"

Samantha's weepy feelings over the beautiful flowers lost out to the gurgle of laughter building in her.

"I love the way you talk," she said finally, allowing the laughter to escape.

Richard's smile changed to one of deep tenderness. "I hope that's not all you love about me."

Samantha hesitated. "No, Richard. I don't think it is."

She placed the flowers on the dashboard and put the truck into reverse. As she backed out, planning to head to the mall, she admitted to herself that that wasn't the only thing she loved about him at all.

# *Chapter Nine*

"I grew up in Hill Creek, actually," Samantha said as their food arrived.

Richard said grace and then continued to grill her. "Has the town grown much?"

Samantha finished her own prayer and lifted her head. Eyes twinkling, she smiled. "Yes, it has. When I was in grade school we were all in one building. But by fourth grade we got our new high school."

She took a bite of her meaty dish and chewed. When she was done, she continued, "Just this past year we opened a middle school."

"That's the new building I passed on the outskirts of town? Large, sprawling and brick?"

She nodded. "We had temporary buildings at both the elementary and the high school. We should have built the middle school a good three years before. In the past seven years Hill Creek has boomed. We're easily over twenty thousand now."

Richard grinned. "Thirty thousand is what I hear around town."

"What?" Samantha asked, tilting her head slightly, her fork paused over her dish of chicken.

"Thirty thousand sounds so small. Twenty thousand even smaller."

"When I was growing up it was about five thousand."

The ambience in the restaurant was just what he'd hoped for: low lights, soft music, Spanish lyrics, and a nice semisecluded table.

When they arrived, Richard had asked for an out-of-the-way table because of his ankle. The Mexican hostess had given them a polite smile and led them to a table near some hanging ivy. The wall was decorated with a serape and bottles of various sizes.

"And you?" Samantha cut into his thoughts.

He had been about to take a bite of the steak he'd ordered. He paused. "And me what?"

"Did you grow up in a large town?"

Richard smiled, remembering his hometown. "Actually, no. The town I'm from was about five thousand."

"Aha!" she said, grinning.

"Aha?" he asked.

"You're all put-on," she replied. "You come from a small town just like me."

He dipped his head in acknowledgment. "True."

"So you went to a small school too, then?"

"Not quite."

He took a bite of the steak and chewed.

"What was it like growing up overseas?"

He shrugged. Though it made him uncomfortable to talk with Samantha about it, he thought this might be the opening he'd waited for, to break it to her who he was. "It's different than here in some ways, and then in other ways it's the same. I had friends I played with. My grandparents and parents were all alive at that time. However, I was sent off to school and boarded there."

"Boarding school?" Samantha asked.

He nodded. "Then my father moved to America. My father and I had a huge falling-out and I swore never to come over here. But I did. I came over and attended college. I wanted nothing to do with him at the time. He wasn't a Christian and so we certainly didn't see eye to eye on faith. And my mom had died by then in America and I blamed him for bringing her over here.''

"I'm sorry," Samantha said. She reached across the table and touched his hand that held the knife.

He laid it down and then turned his hand up, catching her palm. "There's no reason to be. My mother was a Christian. And later I found out that while I was away in college, my father became a Christian. But by that time I was drifting from God, so our relationship was a bit strained for other reasons.''

He chuckled and shook his head. Releasing Samantha's hand, he picked his knife back up and used it to cut his meat.

"That's such an English thing,'' Samantha said.

Richard glanced up at her. "What?''

"You hold your knife in one hand and fork in the other and cut and then put the fork in your mouth without ever putting down your knife.''

"Ah…" he nodded. "There are some things I still do reminiscent of the old world."

"I guess switching hands to cut meat is a new world thing."

He shrugged. "Most countries don't do it."

"I see it on the news sometimes, oddities like that when the media catches state dinners overseas or the such."

He grinned.

"So, do you get along with your father now?" Samantha asked before taking another bite of her chicken.

He nodded. "Better than in the past. I'm still closer to my grandda because he's the one who spent so much of my childhood with me and actually led me to the Lord."

"Grandda? I don't think I've ever heard anyone use that word."

The opening he'd been waiting for. Richard set his knife and fork down. Reaching across the table he took Samantha's hand. "I need to tell you something, Samantha, and I'm not sure how."

She blinked. Then that wonderful honest smile curved her lips, lighting up her eyes. "Just spit it out, then."

"Since I've met you, you've turned my life upside down. I think you realize that."

Samantha smiled, though he saw nervousness enter her eyes.

"In more ways than one, I imagine," she chuckled.

He rubbed his thumb over the tops of her hands. "I've enjoyed every single way," he said softly.

Her nervousness fled and her eyes turned soft. "I have too. Richard, I can't tell you how much you mean to me. It's as if it's too good to be true—like in some fairy tale, you've come and swept me totally off my feet."

Richard's heart expanded at her words. "And you have done the same to me. I feel like, since meeting you, my world has turned on its axis. I was simply walking along in life, existing, wondering what was next. I thought things in my life needed to change. It was time and then, *voilà,* there you were, running me over. And you still are, with your honesty and innocence and gentleness."

"Please," she said, averting her gaze, embarrassed.

"Look at me," Richard commanded softly.

When she finally lifted her shy gaze back to his, he continued. "I wouldn't hurt you for the world. I can't emphasize that enough."

She nodded. "I believe you."

"Then, I want to tell you about my family some more. Will you listen?"

"Of course I will—"

"Hello, Samantha."

Startled, Richard heard the male voice by their table. He released her hands, glancing up as he did.

A man in his mid-fifties stood there. Tall, wide shoulders, some gray peppering his dark hair—Richard realized the man would be considered nice-looking to a woman. He looked vaguely familiar, he thought.

He watched Samantha's reaction.

She withdrew her hands from the table, slipping them under the tablecloth. The sweet smile on her face and the light in her eyes faded to be replaced by a guarded look as her gaze held that of the man who stood before her.

"Hello, Dad."

Stunned, Richard didn't say a word.

*Dad?*

So, this was the man who left her when she was seven.

"I'm in town heading up a construction project. My— Stephen and I were in here eating and I saw you sitting here and thought I'd say hi."

Samantha nodded. "It's the first time I've been here. I usually eat over at the diner."

"I saw it was still there."

"Yes." She didn't elaborate.

He shifted slightly. "Well then, tell Granny hi."

She nodded. "Tell your son hi."

"I just wanted to see you."

"Well, you have," she replied.

"Okay. Well." He nodded to Richard and then turned and headed back across the room to a table not too far away. At it sat a young man, maybe five years younger than Samantha. A young woman sat with them as well.

"Your father left when you were a child," Richard said.

Samantha picked up her fork and started eating. "I don't see him very often." She shrugged but still wouldn't look at him.

"You have a brother?"

She shook her head. "He has a son, from his second marriage."

Light dawned. "I see."

"Yes. Named Stephen. My dad married when I was still seven. Six months after he divorced my mom. Supposedly, his new wife helped straighten his life all out. Of course, I didn't know any of this at the time. I was seventeen when I next saw him again."

"Ten years," Richard said.

She nodded. "I walked into the store from visiting Granny at the hospital and he was standing there with my mom. It seems she'd heard from him several times over the years, but hadn't thought to let me know."

Richard could hear the hurt in Samantha's voice and wanted to take it away, but he didn't know how.

"I found out that he was there to talk to my mom. Mom blew up because I was home early from the hospital. She didn't want me to have anything to do with him. Most likely she hadn't wanted me to know about the meeting either. She was always bilking the store for money and I guess she was afraid I might strike out against him that he never sent us any money, you know.

Like some kids get. What she didn't know was that I didn't want anything to do with him, so her anger over me seeing him was a moot point.

"Of course, Mom screamed at him and told him to go. And he did, without a word to me. She told me then about his other family. He'd supposedly been having an affair and got a woman pregnant. He left us for his new family, but had never gotten over Mom, she said.''

Richard reached out and touched Samantha's hand. Pain pierced his heart as he watched his lovely Samantha experience a wide variety of emotions as she told the story.

"I don't care. I didn't need him anyway.'' She shrugged. ''But it did hurt at the time.''

"Of course,'' Richard agreed.

"That's why I absolutely hate lies. I grew up living with my parents' lies. I swore to do my best never to lie and never to be around anyone who lied.''

"Your mom lied to you?'' Richard wasn't sure what she meant.

"About everything. She was an alcoholic. She would swear to me she didn't have liquor in the house and was off it, and then I'd find a bottle. Or I'd wake up and find her passed out drunk on the living room floor. The first time was the night Daddy left us. Of course, it continued.''

Samantha sighed. Releasing Richard's hand, she lifted both of hers to her cheeks. ''I'm sorry, Richard. I didn't want to discuss this. My dad throws me for a loop whenever I see him.''

Richard nodded. Her father had actually seemed pleasant, if a bit hesitant, as he'd approached Sam. ''Have you ever talked to your dad about the anger you have toward him?''

Samantha shook her head. ''I have no desire to speak with him.''

Richard wasn't willing to push it. ''So, where were we?'' he asked, trying to gather his thoughts and change the subject from her dad. It was obviously a sore spot for her.

''You were about to tell me about your family.''

Richard paused, then memory came rushing back about what he had been about to confess. He was a Dunnington.

She hated lies.

He hadn't lied, he argued with himself. It just hadn't come up.

But would she see it that way?

Her eyes kept darting toward the other table. This didn't bode well.

He had to hope he would be able to tell Samantha when she was in a better mood. But he couldn't sit on this information after hearing her story.

"Well, actually, Sam," he began hesitantly. "It's not about my family exactly. It's about me."

Richard noted that as Samantha's dad and his son got up and left, along with the woman, Samantha visibly relaxed.

She smiled, seeming to soften some as she returned her attention to Richard. "Then, I want to hear it."

"Well, we'll see," he replied and chuckled. Realizing how nervous he was, he actually cleared his throat. "You see, I'm Richard—"

"Hi!"

Richard choked on his words.

*Not again.*

Richard glanced at Angela and another lovely lady.

Samantha patiently turned to them. "Hello, Laura. Angie."

"I dragged Mom over here because she is planning a get-together at her house and I told her that she had to stop by the store and get some of your specialty items.''

Laura smiled. ''I hope we're not interrupting.''

Richard wanted to say, *yes!* But instead, he left the conversation to Samantha.

His Samantha, who was too sweet to be rude. ''Not at all. I can always talk business.''

She cast a quick apologetic look at Richard. He smiled.

A few months ago, he would have done the same had someone come up and wanted to discuss work with him. And he knew Samantha needed the business. ''Please, have a seat,'' he found himself saying.

Standing, he pulled both chairs out for the women before reseating himself. ''I'm Richard, Samantha's boarder,'' he replied.

Laura held out her hand and he shook it.

And then he sat back and spent the rest of his date discussing candy and baby showers.

# *Chapter Ten*

"It's been three weeks!"

Richard, who walked through Dunnington's inspecting the stock that was already in the store even though construction wasn't done, leaned on his cane and nodded. "I know how long it's been. I tried to tell her, several times. I swear something is keeping me from it. Every time I set her up to explain, someone interrupts or stops by or just has to talk with her."

Dillon sighed. "That's the American way. If you really want to tell her, you're going to have to simply pull her into a back room, close the door, ignore the interruptions and tell her."

Richard nodded. "You know, I was angry with

my fiancée when I found out the way I did about her other engagement. I see now that I was so busy, we never had any time alone.''

Dillon sighed. ''It wasn't meant to be, bud.''

''I know that now. I think I knew that then. My dad wanted it more than I did. I was angry that she hadn't bothered to tell me before announcing it, though.''

''Just like this woman is going to be really angry if this store opens in three weeks and she doesn't know who you are until you're cutting the ribbon.''

Richard sighed wearily. ''I want to ask her to marry me.''

Dillon turned red in the face. An outsider might think he was having a stroke. Or a fit.

Richard knew that Dillon was simply reacting to Richard's words.

''Tell her.''

''I'm going to—''

''Excuse me.''

Both men turned to see who had spoken.

Richard immediately recognized the construction worker as Samantha's father, Stephen.

''Yes?'' Dillon said, a bit put out at being interrupted.

"Mr. Moore. I wanted to speak with you, if I may?"

"Mr. Moore—" Dillon began.

Richard waved him off. "I have time." Glancing at Dillon, he asked, "Are the offices upstairs completed yet?"

"Yeah," Dillon replied. "And I'll be in mine when you're done here."

Dillon's curious gaze ran over the man before he turned and left.

Richard smoothed the lapel of his gray jacket where it V'd down to the button at his waist. Then he took the cane and started walking toward the elevators. "This way," he replied.

The man looked only momentarily confused before he shrugged and followed Richard.

Neither said anything in the elevator. When it opened, Richard turned right and traveled the length of the hall, past the finished offices.

At the last door, he shoved it opened. "Mr. Moore! So nice to finally see you," the secretary said. "I'd heard you were in town."

"I'm not to be disturbed," he said shortly, and then entered the office. He closed the door behind them both.

Turning, he held out his hand. "Richard Moore," he said.

"Stephen Hampton."

"Senior?" Richard asked.

"I see you've heard Samantha's version of my story."

Richard turned and made his way across the room to a sofa. He motioned for Stephen to have a seat. "I've heard some."

Stephen sat down gingerly on the plush brown leather chair that sat at an angle to the sofa.

"So, how may I help you?"

"We're on schedule again. We should be finished next week with the rest of the store."

Richard nodded. Stephen had aged well. Over the past three weeks, Samantha had talked more and more about her father. Richard found out he was only forty-nine. He'd evidently had her a year after he and Samantha's mom married. He had no wrinkles, his face was smooth and clear. The only indication of age was the gray hair, which had originally caused Richard to guess him older than he was. But with the hard hat on right now, he looked younger.

"Since you don't normally report to me, I can

assume you wanted to talk to me about your daughter and that was simply an icebreaker?''

The older man dropped his gaze. He allowed his hands to hang loose between his knees. ''How well do you know my daughter?''

Richard lifted an eyebrow.

Stephen shifted. ''I'm not trying to be paternal or anything. I just meant, well, I needed some advice. You two looked really cozy the other night and I thought maybe you could help me.''

Richard studied the man with an inscrutable stare. ''Just what is it you want?''

The man shifted again. Finally, softly, he said, ''I want to know my daughter.''

Ah.

Stephen glanced around the office, out the window, anywhere but directly at Richard.

When he wouldn't meet Richard's gaze, Richard finally asked, ''Why?''

That brought the man's gaze around to his. ''Because she's my daughter!''

''She was your daughter twenty-some odd years ago when you left her too,'' Richard said. ''So what's changed?''

''It's not really any of your business,'' the man said.

Richard's gaze hardened. "Nor is your daughter's business yours."

The older man reached up and ran a weary hand down his face. "It'd be easier if I knew where you stood with her," he muttered.

Richard felt the soft fluttery feeling deep down inside him and knew it was the Holy Spirit prompting him. It was a soft, gentle voice, but nonetheless His voice, as He whispered to Richard's heart. *Be honest with him.*

Richard had spent almost all of his spare time the past three weeks reading the Bible and praying, drawing closer to God. Had he not been, he doubted he would have heeded that voice within him.

Now, however, he only hesitated a moment before he said, "I love your daughter very much."

The man's worry melted from his face and his shoulders slumped in relief. "I thought so. My daughter has been so caught up in the business, even when she was a little tike, that she's rarely dated. It's been different with you."

"How would you know?" Richard hadn't asked it in an accusatory tone. He had a feeling, however, from what Stephen had just said, that he was missing something big in the story behind

Sam's parents' divorce—something Samantha wasn't aware of either.

"I've kept tabs on her since the day I left, that's how."

Richard sat still after that small bomb was dropped. He didn't move, didn't question the man, but just stared at him, waiting.

Finally the man said, "I guess I'm going to have to explain everything to gain your trust."

Richard simply nodded.

"Samantha's mom and I divorced when Samantha was seven. Samantha's mom had become a lush and I'd found out she'd had an affair. She and I didn't see eye to eye. Right after our marriage, I discovered she'd had an abortion and I wasn't too happy with her. Well, she was pregnant with Sam by the time I found out, so we decided to stick it out. But Samantha's mom didn't like the fact that I worked for someone in construction. Her mom was a business owner and I was simply a construction worker—at least back then I was. By the time Samantha was four years old, her mom was bitterly disappointed in me."

Stephen rubbed his eyes. "Samantha's grandparents were one of the founding families of Hill Creek. They were well respected. They could pay off any scandal their daughter created, including her sleeping around. By the time Samantha was six, her mom was drinking heavily. I gave her an ultimatum—stop drinking or I would leave her.''

"You left Samantha with someone like that?'' Richard asked, thinking the man more than a little irresponsible.

Stephen spread his hands. ''There was no way I could get custody. Her grandfather told me that if I tried, he'd drag my name through the mud and make sure I never had a job again. I didn't have the money to fight her family—they used to have money. Anyway, the thought of putting Samantha through a nasty custody battle when I knew there was no way to win was not to my liking.

"I thought it'd end there. I would leave and in time Shellie would realize she didn't want the child and I'd get custody. Only, Sam's grandfather made sure I couldn't get her. He filed desertion papers and managed to see that Shellie got full custody.''

"You could have tried.''

Stephen shook his head. ''Back then, mothers almost always got the custody of their children. It's not like today when a man can actually get his kid. Anyway, through different circumstances, Samantha's grandparents lost most of their money. It wasn't long before I got a letter from Shellie demanding money to take care of Samantha.''

Richard leaned forward. This was something he hadn't expected. ''And?'' he prompted.

''I wrote her back insisting that if I sent her money, I wanted regular reports sent to me by the local attorney on how she was doing. I knew Shellie was a drunk. I still had a couple of sources in Hill Creek. But they all said that Granny took good care of Samantha.''

Bitterly, Stephen added, ''I didn't realize how they'd warped my child against me or the fact that she was being hurt so much by my ex-wife's drinking.''

''You remarried. Why didn't you try to get custody then, claiming you had a steady income and a good household to bring her to?''

Stephen sighed. ''I should have. Hindsight is always twenty-twenty. I'd been gone three years by then and thought, at the time, that it'd do more harm, fighting to get her out of the house. It wasn't until my new wife led me to the Lord when Samantha was seventeen that I decided I didn't care what Samantha's family did to me. Being a Christian can change a person's outlook in so many ways. And it did me. I wanted to see her.''

A strange compassion flooded Richard. After listening to Samantha's bitterness, he hadn't thought twice about this man, but now, having heard Stephen Hampton's story, he realized Samantha had no idea what had really happened.

''But by then I'd found out that Samantha hated me and wanted nothing to do with me. Her grandmother had just had a stroke, and as far as Sammie was concerned, I was the devil incarnate.''

Richard smiled slightly.

''What?'' Stephen asked.

He shook his head, not about to tell the man that was the very term Samantha had unknowingly applied to him.

''I've tried to talk to her several times. I have all of the reports the lawyer sent me over the years. I've kept track of her, even coming by to see her when she didn't know that I was around. But I just can't get her to listen. Whenever I get near her, she turns all cold.''

''And you want me to talk to her?'' Richard asked.

"I'm not sure what I want," Stephen admitted.

Richard frowned. He was opening his mouth to comment when his cell phone rang.

"Excuse me," he said, and pulled the small silver unit from his pocket.

"Hello?"

"Richard, it's me."

The fear in Samantha's voice alarmed him. Over the weeks he'd come to discover a compassionate and loving woman in his Samantha, one who had a temper and could play a mean hand of spades. But never had he heard fear. That was what he heard now.

"What is it, honey?" he asked gently, trying to make his voice soothing. "I'm here."

"Oh, Richard," Samantha said on a sob. "It's Granny. She's had another stroke. And I don't think she's doing very well."

Granny had been Samantha's stable oak in the midst of the storm. Samantha was falling apart at the thought of losing her. It was in her voice.

"Where are you?" Richard demanded. "I'll be right there."

"I'm at the hospital. It's just south of town."

He nodded. "Give me five minutes."

He snapped the phone closed and looked up at

Samantha's father. "I'll see you get paid for the rest of the day plus a bonus if you can drive me somewhere."

"Okay," Stephen said, looking confused. His puzzlement faded, however, when Richard continued.

"That was Sam. Granny's had a stroke and it doesn't look good."

Stephen stood. "Where are they?"

"The hospital," Richard replied.

He grabbed his cane and together they left, determination in their stride as they rushed to the side of the woman they both loved.

# Chapter Eleven

Samantha was having trouble breathing. She knew tears were useless, but when she'd gone to get Granny up this morning and she hadn't budged…

It had terrified her.

And that terror was still with her as she paced the emergency room now.

When Richard came rushing into the ER, she threw herself into his arms and burst into tears. ''I'm so scared, Richard,'' she cried, and clung to him.

Richard's arms went around her, pulling her safely into his warmth.

She trembled as he held her.

"What happened?" Richard's voice rumbled against the side of her face, its deep tones giving her the courage to confess the story.

"I went up to wake Granny for breakfast just before the home-health nurse arrived. Granny wouldn't move." Samantha gasped as a new sob escaped. "I shook her, thinking she was…was… just sleeping." Samantha shuddered and wrapped her arms tightly around Richard. "But—but she di-didn't wa-wake up."

She felt Richard's hand stroke her head, down her hair, and she shuddered.

"It's okay, honey. Shh now," he whispered.

Samantha ached. "I must have been screaming or something. Angela came running. She called the ambulance. She stayed at the store for me. I guess she opened it. I don't know. Maybe she didn't. She had to be at school sometime…"

Samantha couldn't even recall when Angela went to school. Thinking was a near impossibility.

"It doesn't matter right now," Richard soothed her. "Has a doctor been out to talk to you yet?"

Samantha shook her head.

"I'll see what I can find out."

Samantha knew that voice. Pulling back, she looked around and saw her father standing there, hard hat under his arm. "What are you doing here?" Samantha asked.

Stephen flinched at the acid in her voice. She couldn't help it, however. The last person she had expected to see was her dad. She watched as he cast a look at Richard and then hurried toward the receptionist.

Her gaze lifted to Richard's. "What is he doing here?"

Richard kept his arm around her as he turned her and led her over to a chair. "Your dad came to see me this morning. We had a long talk."

Samantha tried to pull away but Richard wouldn't let her.

"He told me the entire story of what happened between him and your mom."

"I know what happened," Samantha said, shaking, feeling betrayed that Richard had been talking to her father behind her back.

"No, honey, I don't think you do."

Stephen returned. "They're still working on her," he said.

"What do you care?" Samantha said hatefully, striking out in hurt.

"I'd better go," Stephen said.

Richard shook his head. "I think you'd better tell her what you told me," he countered.

Stephen hesitated.

"I don't want to hear it." Samantha tried to pull away again.

"Yes, you do," Richard replied gently.

She glared up at her father, unable to believe he stood there looking vulnerable. It was she who was vulnerable, not he. How dare he look at her like that when he was the one who'd ruined their family?

"Stephen," Richard prompted.

Samantha opened her mouth.

"Just hear him out," Richard said.

"I've never left you, really," Stephen said.

Rage bubbled up in Samantha. "That's a lie. You walked out when I was seven and I didn't see you for ten years. How can you say you didn't leave me?"

He sighed. "I mean—"

"She's old enough to hear the truth," Richard interrupted.

Stephen shrugged. "It's no secret your mom and I had problems. What you didn't know, honey, was that she was having an affair on me."

"You liar!"

Stephen shook his head. "I moved out and was going to file for divorce. Before I could, your grandfather filed desertion charges and made sure I never had custody of you."

"They wouldn't do that," Samantha cried. She couldn't believe that her dad would choose to come back into her life and tell her all of this right now, when she was going through so much with Granny.

"Yes. They did. They loved their daughter. They had the money and they didn't like that I was only a construction worker. They hadn't from day one. That doesn't mean, however, that they didn't love you. Granny and Grandpa doted on you."

"So tell me something new," she replied nastily. She didn't want to hear this. Not now.

But Richard's arm kept her anchored there. As much as she wanted to get up and run from the story, she didn't want to lose Richard's warmth. She held on to his forearm where it encircled her waist.

"I demanded reports from the family lawyer. He agreed. I came by when I could, but wasn't allowed to see you. They'd made it sound as if I might kidnap you, and honestly, back then, I might have. But then I found the Lord, when you were seventeen. I decided I had to come clean, so I came to tell you...but Granny was in the hospital with a stroke and I found out then just how much their lies had affected you. You hated me.''

Samantha hated him now. Hated him for telling her this. A Christian? Her daddy couldn't be a Christian. He had left her. ''Mom said you were having an affair and the woman was pregnant.''

Stephen shook his head. ''Stephen Junior wasn't born until a year and a half after I remarried.''

The woman she had hated for years that had stolen her daddy hadn't been pregnant? And Stephen wasn't the same age as she was? She shook her head, trying to make sense of what she'd thought she knew and what her father was telling her now.

What her father had said won out as the information seeped into her mind. If the woman hadn't been pregnant, then her mom had lied to her. So had Granny. No, Granny had never said that. Though she had said everything was better the way it was.

She shook her head.

''When we got the news, I brought Richard

over here. He's right. It's time you know the truth, honey. I wanted to tell you when you were seventeen but it just didn't work out. I've approached you several times over the years, but you wouldn't listen.''

''Why now?'' Samantha asked, and leaned her head against Richard. She couldn't believe all she was hearing. Mind-numbing facts that she couldn't deal with right now, not with Granny in there fighting for her life.

''Because you have someone who loves you more than life and he's willing to make sure you don't live with any more lies.''

Richard stiffened.

Samantha glanced up at him. Had she not been so upset, she would have asked why Richard looked so tense. Instead, her mind took in those words her father had said.

''He told you he loved me?''

''It's obvious,'' her father said gruffly.

''You know I do,'' Richard said, and reached up with his free hand to cup her cheek. ''That's why I came running as soon as you called. I love you, Samantha.''

''I don't want her to die,'' Samantha whispered

so forlornly that she realized she sounded like a small child.

She *felt* like a small child. "She's been the only stability in my life, Richard. At least before, Granny could look at me when she had her strokes. This time she didn't even move, her eyes never met mine."

"She'll be okay," Richard whispered.

"I'm not leaving you this time," Stephen added. "I'm staying here for you. And when I go back over to Hilton," he said, mentioning one of the nearby towns, "I am going to make sure you don't lose me and I don't lose you."

She heard her father but kept her eyes on Richard. "I don't want to lose you either."

"Never," he whispered. He leaned down and kissed her on the head. "Have you called the pastor?" he asked.

She shook her head.

"He's a good man. I'm sure he'd want to be here—"

"I'll call," Stephen interrupted.

Richard gave him the name of the church, and Stephen hurried over to the pay phone.

"Why did you bring him here?" Samantha asked, now that he was gone.

"He gave me a ride. I was over at the mall when I got the call. He was there. Besides, Sam, when he told me the story, I knew you had to know the truth."

She pushed back slightly. Staring across the room at her dad, she said, "I can't believe it. I mean, all my life I've been told he left us because his new wife was pregnant. When I found out he had another child, I knew he didn't want me. I always wondered why. When I found out he had a son, I was ten years old. And I thought that was it. He'd left us because I was a girl. I hated him, Richard. I can't believe he really was checking up on me."

"How did you find out when you were ten?" Richard asked.

"Mom told me." She paused. "Mom told me," she repeated, "which means she was probably in touch with him."

Richard rubbed his hand up and down her arm. "He said that after your grandparents lost most of their wealth, your mom demanded money to raise you."

"She what?" Samantha lifted wide eyes to Richard.

Richard nodded. "I'm sure it could be verified

through the lawyer. If he's not still around, then a private investigator could dig up the information for you.''

''But she was always broke,'' Samantha argued. ''We never had money for me to do anything when I was growing up—especially after Granny had the first stroke.''

''Alcoholism is a very expensive sin,'' Richard said gently.

Fresh tears filled Samantha's eyes. ''What have...I believed...all of these years?'' she asked brokenly.

Leaning back into Richard, she simply clung to him as her mind reeled. Richard continued explaining everything her dad had told him earlier, until she was certain she was going to break into pieces hearing about all of the lies and half-truths she'd been living with over the years.

''There's more,'' Richard said.

Samantha felt him straighten as he said that. However, with the way she felt, she thought if she had even one more tiny piece of information, she was going to shatter. She just couldn't hear it. Not right now, at least.

She shook her head. ''Please. I can't take any more right now.''

"I really need to tell you," Richard said.

She could hear the tension in his voice—as strong as the tension that ran down her spine, tightening it until she felt as if it would snap in half.

"I've been trying to tell you for three weeks, actually, since the day I met you."

She shook her head. "I just can't," she replied. "Not until I know Granny is okay."

"The pastor is on his way," Stephen said as he returned to their side. "How is she?"

She wanted to lash out again at him for asking. How many years had he ignored her...but then, if what he and Richard said was true, she hadn't been ignored all those years.

She couldn't say anything, not right now, not to Richard and not to her father. She was only grateful Richard was here to hold her and offer comfort while they waited on news.

A sudden flurry of people rushing into the ER had Samantha pulling back. "What's going on?"

Doctors and nurses sprinted past.

"An accident, maybe?" Richard offered, glancing up and trying to see if anyone new had come in.

"I can't tell," Stephen said, craning his neck.

A sinking feeling slipped into Samantha's stomach, turning it and expanding it until she felt as if she was going to throw up. Looking up helplessly at Richard, she simply waited. She knew the medical personnel weren't there for someone else. They'd come rushing to the ER because of Granny.

She couldn't voice it, though. As the minutes ticked past and even after the pastor arrived, she could only stare at Richard. He stared back at her, not breaking her gaze, silently offering support.

When she saw Julian walk through the door, she knew.

She felt every bit of blood drain from her face. Carefree Julian who so loved life had the look of defeat on his face.

''No.'' She shook her head, not wanting to hear it.

As she did, Sheriff Mitch McCade came walking in. ''Hey, Julian,'' he said.

''Just a minute,'' Julian said to his brother.

Mitch looked from Julian to Samantha. His features darkened. Oh, he knew all right, what his brother was about to say. It was there in his look. Samantha clamped hard onto Richard's arm.

Together, they stood.

"I'm sorry, Sam. We did everything we could."

"No," she repeated. Trembling, she stared in denial at Julian. "You're wrong."

Julian reached out and squeezed her shoulder. "You know I wouldn't lie to you," he replied.

Samantha turned and threw herself into Richard's arms.

Richard willingly took the brunt of her pain as he wrapped both arms around her. The sound that came from her mouth was like that of a wounded animal. Richard hurt, literally aching, as he held her; her grief was so vivid.

Stephen moved forward and began to rub her back. Tears were in his eyes.

Julian looked up at Richard. "Her heart just quit. We tried to get her back. The ER doctor was working on her when I got here. It was just her time."

Samantha cried out louder in Richard's arms. He gently rocked her back and forth, back and forth.

Mitch had walked up and stood there by his brother, hat in hand, frown on his face. This was a close-knit community and one person's death affected them all. Richard remembered his grandma's death and how everyone had known her. Mitch looked stricken by the death as well. Though he didn't know the man, Richard appreciated the fact that Mitch cared about his Samantha.

"Thank you," Richard said to Julian. "I'll make sure she understands that."

Julian turned to Mitch. "What did you need?"

Mitch waved a hand toward Richard. "I needed to speak with Mr. Moore. His secretary said he'd rushed over here to the hospital. I didn't know why at the time."

"What is it?" Richard asked, wondering what in the world the sheriff needed him for.

"There's been a small fire at Dunnington's."

Richard stiffened, feeling his features freeze as he realized what Mitch had just revealed.

"Seems one of the construction crew's tools overheated and shorted out. It's contained to only part of the store," he continued. Mitch had no idea that Samantha was hearing every word, or that she didn't know who Richard was. When Richard didn't say anything, Mitch continued.

"You are Richard Moore, right? Angela pointed you out the other day. Dillon said you

were in charge and that you'd know what was to
be done. Since your secretary said you were over
here, I thought I'd give you the news in person.''

Slowly, the woman in his arms tensed.

Confused, Mitch looked from him, to Samantha, to Stephen. Julian, who had started to walk
off, had paused and was watching the scene
closely as well.

''Your last name isn't Dunnington,'' Samantha
said, looking up at Richard. ''What is he talking
about?''

Mitch's gaze suddenly hardened. Though Julian
tried to remain neutral, he fleetingly saw disap-
proval in his gaze. Samantha's dad simply gog-
gled at them, as the truth dawned on him.

''My mother is a Dunnington.''

The look in her eyes had him rushing on. ''But
that's not important right now. That's what I had
to tell you. From the first night we met.''

''You set me up,'' she accused.

''Huh?'' Richard stared at her, not sure what
she meant.

''The store. I'm competition. It was so easy.
You found out who I was. Why not take an apartment? Learn all of my secrets. It'd be easier to
put me out of business, wouldn't it?''

She jerked back from him, stumbling.

He reached for her.

Samantha threw her hands up. "Don't touch me!" Her breathing became labored. "Don't come near me! How could you!"

"It's not like that, Sam!" He'd expected a reaction, but just a little anger, not this awful reaction.

Fear clenched his gut. He reached for her and then dropped his hands, realizing he didn't dare touch her with that look on her face. "I tried to tell you. I just...kept on getting interrupted," he finished lamely. Oh, what a lie that was, he suddenly realized. He should have done as Dillon had said—taken her to the back room, locked the door and told her.

But he was so caught up in those feelings of love that he hadn't thought telling her was such a big deal. Oh, she'd be angry, but when he explained, they would laugh about it and then he could give her some ideas on how to boost sales.

"I wanted to help you."

"Help me?" she demanded. She was losing it. Her breath now came out in short gasps.

Mitch's gaze was on her as he eased forward.

Concern etched his features. "Calm down, honey," he said quietly. "Let him explain."

"Explain?" she asked, turning wild eyes on Mitch. "Explain?" She covered her mouth with her hand and started laughing.

Julian had now turned back to her, concerned. "Get me 1 cc of Ativan," he said to a nearby nurse.

Samantha threw her hands up in the air. "Sure, let him explain how he lived under my roof and lied to me. Just like my mom, my dad and my grandmother. Just like everyone else! Let's see him explain his way out of that!"

She started laughing again. And then she turned intending to run, but instead she ran right into a plant that decorated the waiting room.

Thrown off balance, she fell.

Mitch beat Richard to her, catching her in his arms.

"Leave me alone! Just everyone leave me alone," she cried.

Richard started forward. Mitch shook his head no. Stephen hurried over too.

Samantha started crying hysterically.

The nurse returned with the shot. Julian

swabbed a spot on her arm and gave her the sedative.

Samantha didn't stop crying.

Mitch scooped her limp and hysterical form like a broken doll, into his arms. "Where do you want her?" he said to Julian.

"Room three," Julian said, and led the way.

Mitch called over his shoulder to the nurse. "Call my wife. Sam needs someone right now."

And then they were out of sight.

Reeling, Richard simply stared.

"Is it true what she said? Are you here to put her out of business?"

Slowly, Richard turned to the only other person in the waiting room. Stephen stood there. Surprisingly enough, he didn't appear judgmental.

He shrugged at Richard's look. "I know how easy it is to jump to wrong conclusions."

Richard shook his head. "My only mistake is falling in love before she knew who I was."

Stephen's mouth twisted into a grimace.

Richard continued. "I don't know why it didn't come out that first night, but then, later, I thought she'd simply get over it. It was never intentional."

"It never is—hurting a person we love," he

said, and Richard saw the yearning in his eyes for his daughter.

"Yeah," Richard replied.

His phone rang again and he answered. "Hello?"

"It's me, Dillon. There's been a small fire. I needed to talk to you about it…"

"Not now, Dillon." He simply shut the phone, snapping it closed and then turning it off.

"So, what are you going to do now?" Stephen asked.

Richard sat down in one of the chairs and dropped his hands between his knees. Feeling much older than he actually was, he said, "I'm going to sit here and pray—and hope that when Sam calms down, she'll let me back into her life."

Stephen hesitated. Then he walked over, sat down next to Richard and said, "That sounds like a good idea, son."

Together they bowed their heads and prayed that the woman in their lives would be okay.

# Chapter Twelve

"Well, that's it. It looks like we made enough maybe to last until July," said Samantha. The store was closed. Twilight was approaching.

And today had been an incredibly slow—and sad—day for the candy store.

Angela clasped her hands, studying her friend worriedly. "Well, look at the bright side," she said, and grinned, hoping to entice her friend into a smile. "If we do a big promotion for July, then maybe that'll last us until the fall."

Samantha sat back from the small wooden table and shoved the ledger aside. The wind was whipping up loudly outside, rattling the windows in the other room. Inside, however, the cold didn't affect them. A fire roared in the fireplace. It was only Samantha who seemed to be frozen inside, Angela thought.

"Except that Dunnington's is opening July Fourth." Samantha sighed into the unusual silence. "Why was I so determined to keep this candy shop, Angie?"

Angela was careful with how she responded. Her friend had been a mass of emotions since Granny's passing two months ago. Now, today, the first of April, she had regretfully dismissed the other employees, cutting the staff to only her, Angela and Mary. Angela only wished she could say this all was an April fool, but she'd seen the ledgers herself.

"You loved the work," Angela said quietly, not daring to bring up what she most wanted to talk with Samantha about, not wanting to mention Richard's name.

"Did I?" Samantha looked around the store. "Or did I love that it was something to hold on to after my father left? Granny took me under her wing and trained me in making the candy and running the store."

"You know you love it." Angela tried to encourage her, though she wasn't sure Samantha loved anything anymore. The smell of this morning's burned batch of butter brickle still filled the air, telling her that it was simply a job, nothing more, nothing sweet about it at all. The store was something that had soured since Samantha found out the truth about her family. The smell reminded them of that now.

"I admit I love making the candy. Getting to experiment with all of the different flavors... finding new recipes...that's the fun part."

"And you're always coming up with some great new ideas."

Samantha sighed. "Let's face it. I'm just not a businessperson. While Granny could still make the decisions, the store held its own, but since I took over it has been in steady decline. I'm just no good at promoting and bringing the customers in and keeping them coming back for more."

"Your candy does that."

"Well, yes," Samantha admitted, to Angie's relief. "But only to a point," she added, dashing Angie's hope that she had helped cheer her employer.

"The store needs to be pulled into the twenty-first century. It needs a new look, something that will bring newcomers in, and I just don't know what to do. I don't know if I even want to worry about getting customers anymore, actually.''

''That's just depression talking,'' Angela admonished. ''It's only been two months since…'' Her voice trailed off.

Samantha sighed. ''Since Granny died? Since I found out all of the lies my life has been based on, or since I found out the love I'd discovered was also founded on a falsehood?''

Angela nibbled her lip. Finally, she said, ''I have a confession to make.'' When Samantha didn't say anything, she continued, ''I went out with Dillon a few nights ago.''

Samantha nodded. ''I'm not surprised.''

Relief flooded Angie. ''You're not?''

She shook her head. ''You and he have been hanging out together the past few weeks.''

Angie frowned. She hadn't realized Samantha had noticed. ''Dillon and I are just friends. Besides, Dillon is worried about you.''

Samantha's smile left. ''Richard is sending Dillon to check up on me, isn't he?''

Defensively, Angela replied, ''Well, if you'd simply take one of his calls or not turn your back on him when he tries to talk with you…''

Samantha shook her head. ''He lied to me.

And, unless you haven't noticed, he hasn't called or attempted to see me in a week now.''

The anguish in her whisper broke Angela's heart. "He cares for you, Samantha. I know he does!''

"No. He doesn't, Angie. Do you know, since Granny...since then, he hasn't even been to church.''

"He was at the funeral.''

"But since then, he hasn't attended church once.''

Angela disagreed. "He showed up, but you seemed so upset at seeing him that he found another church.''

"What?'' Samantha stared in surprise at Angela.

Angela hadn't meant for her pronouncement to sound so accusatory. "He goes to the church that Uncle Mitch and Uncle Julian and my dad go to. I saw him there. He told Uncle Mitch that his presence upset you, so he changed churches.''

"What's he doing talking to Mitch?'' Samantha demanded. Agitated, she closed the ledgers and stood. She crossed to the rolltop desk in her living room and shoved the oblong green books inside.

"What? He's not supposed to have friends?"

"But Mitch is my friend!" Samantha argued, and jerked down the rolltop cover. As she did, an envelope fell out.

Angela simply lifted her eyebrows. "Now, that sounded really mature."

Samantha scowled. She bent down and picked up the envelope. Her gaze changed to one of pained recognition.

"What's that?" Angela asked, getting up and crossing to where Samantha stood.

"Nothing."

"It's from Richard," Angela replied, seeing the return address. Taking it from her, she opened the unsealed flap.

Samantha jerked it back. "That's my mail."

"There's a check in there!" Wide-eyed, Angela turned her gaze to Samantha and waited to hear what was going on.

Samantha shrugged and said waspishly, "I'm not cashing it."

"For how much?" she asked, her curiosity going wild.

Samantha just glared at her. When Angela wouldn't back down, she relented. "Six months' worth of rent."

Surprised, Angela stared at Samantha. "But he moved out after Granny's funeral."

She shrugged. "I sent back the rent for the unused month, but he returned it, with this, saying that in most contracts you had to sign at least a six-month lease. If I didn't agree, then he'd be willing to send a year's worth of money. What could I do? If I sent it back, he'd send a year's worth of money to pay me...off." Samantha's voice cracked.

"That's good, isn't it?" Angela didn't get why that upset her so much.

"It's all simply a transaction to him, boiling down to contracts."

Samantha covered her mouth. Turning, she crossed back over to the living room and dropped into a chair. Next to it was a nearly empty box of tissues, and next to that, an overflowing wastebasket. She grabbed a fresh tissue and rubbed her eyes. "I swear I'm not going to shed one more tear over him."

Angela slowly followed. "I don't think Richard thinks of you only as a contract."

"Then, why didn't he bother to tell me who he was?" She waved the envelope at Angie before dropping it on the table next to her.

Angela sighed. They had been over this dozens of times and Samantha simply wasn't going to hear the truth until she was ready. "He tried."

"Not hard enough."

"Just like your dad?" Angela asked.

Samantha shrugged.

"And yet, you're talking to *him* again."

Samantha snatched another tissue and wiped at her eyes. "This is going nowhere. I don't want to talk about it."

Angela sighed, defeated. She had told Dillon she would work on Samantha while he worked on Richard. But it looked like Angela wasn't going to make any headway.

The only good thing she could say was that at least Samantha and her father were talking again.

She tried to imagine what it would have been like, not having a father to talk problems over with all of those years. She simply couldn't comprehend it. As far as she was concerned, she had the best dad in the world, and the best stepmom. Thinking about her stepmom reminded Angela that she and Laura were supposed to meet.

"Laura's probably waiting for me at the diner," Angela said, not wanting to leave but knowing her stepmom was there waiting.

Samantha waved a hand at her. "Go on. I'm going to be fine."

When Angela looked at her dubiously, Samantha shook her head and waved her hand again. "Honestly."

Angela nodded. "Okay, then. If you need a friend, though, call."

Samantha nodded.

As Angela left, Samantha thought that the age difference between the two had never been wider. Angela still had an innocence that believed love conquered all. Samantha knew different. Love hadn't conquered the lies told to her by her mom, or her grandmother and grandfather. It wasn't going to conquer the lies Richard had told her.

*Richard.*

She got up and walked to the front of the store. Going to the window where she could see down the street, she stared at the lighted mall in the settling dusk.

He'd tried to contact her several times. At first she'd been too busy making funeral arrangements to talk with him. She'd also been too angry. Then her dad had approached her. Upset at him, but feeling vulnerable and needing a dad, she had let him back into her life.

Then, later, when Richard would call, she would find an excuse. She was busy with getting reacquainted with her dad or was busy trying to get everything in the store settled or busy trying to handle estate problems.

She had to admit her dad had been sent by God. It was so helpful to have someone with whom she could talk about her grandmother.

And his explanations were a soothing balm to her battered soul. She'd learned so much about him in the past eight weeks. And his family. That part still hurt. She had missed out on years of his life because her mom and her mom's family had been trying to keep her from her dad.

She wasn't sure she could ever forgive them for that.

It was only because of God's grace in her own life that she tried to let it go and get on with life.

Which brought her right back to Richard.

He was still in town. She hadn't been sure the past two or three days if he'd stayed around or given up and left. It'd been nearly a week since he last contacted her.

Not that she wanted him to contact her, she reasoned.

But if he had really loved her, would he have given up as he had?

No.

The truth was that he hadn't really loved her. Deep down she'd known that. It had all been a lie.

He didn't love her. He'd only been scoping out her small store to find out if it was going to be a challenge to shut it down.

Her running him down had been a perfect opportunity for him to make contact. And when she'd offered him somewhere to stay, that had been the icing on the cake.

Still, she remembered his arms around her, the way he held her, his gentle kisses, and his joy as he talked about God.

Lifting her hand to the cold pane of glass, placing it next to where her head rested, she whispered his name longingly.

"Richard."

"You haven't called her." Dillon stood just inside the store manager's office, staring at the man who sat transfixed by one small shop located two blocks from them. Soon enough the store manager would get this office, but until then, while Richard was here, he'd claimed it as his workstation. Dillon thought it had to do with the great view of The Candy Shoppe.

"What's the use?" Richard didn't turn his chair from facing the large glass windows. Instead, he continued to stare, hands steepled in front of him, his gaze directed outward as darkness faded around him.

"She loves you, bud." Dillon hated seeing his friend this way and had decided it was time to attempt to end his self-imposed exile.

"She says she doesn't."

"She hasn't said that," Dillon objected. He knew, nearly by heart, what Samantha had said. He'd heard it enough from Richard and now Angela as well.

Richard sighed. He glanced away from the view and at the refurbished office. Gone was the older furniture. In its place were leather chairs and a sofa, along with cherry-wood credenzas and a cherry-wood desk. The curtains and colors had been changed to yellows and greens, bright and cheery, just the opposite of how Richard felt right now. He only wanted to be left alone to sit here, in the growing darkness, and think about what he had lost. And he might be able to, except for one small problem.

*Dillon.*

Dillon blamed himself for what had happened. Had he gotten to Richard first, he felt he could have avoided the sheriff blurting out the truth.

Richard knew the real truth. It was his own fault for not telling Samantha who he was earlier.

Dillon flipped on the overhead lights before crossing the thick carpet and dropping into one of the plush leather chairs in front of Richard's desk. "Angela said Samantha had to lay off two of her employees today."

Richard sighed. "I'm sure she lays that at my feet as well."

Dillon flipped a leg over the arm of the chair, slumping down. Running his hand up the side of the chair, he tried to act casual as he replied, "Probably. But since when does Dunnington's worry about some store as small as The Candy Shoppe?"

Richard's chair squeaked as he leaned forward. "You know better than that."

Dillon changed the subject. "They've rewired most of the store. Now all they have left to do before we can start stocking again is to re-paint it.''

"My dad is furious over the delay," Richard muttered, leaning back in his chair. Again it creaked.

"Hey, at least they found the problem before we had everything moved in and ended up with a major fire and loss of life. They could have just accepted it was that tool overheating.''

Richard nodded shortly. "We've lost money waiting until July for the grand opening.''

Dillon swung his foot. "We should have just forgotten the store and moved on.''

"Too much advertisement has already gone into this site according to Dad.''

"What does your grandda say?'' Dillon queried.

Richard shrugged. Pulling toward him a sheaf of papers that should have been done hours ago, he said, "He thinks this should be a foundation store for branches out into the West.''

Dillon whistled. "What made him decide that?''

Richard ignored the question, piquing Dillon's curiosity. Instead of pursuing it, he left it for later.

Richard reached for the papers in front of him and scanned the top one.

"How did Samantha look?" he asked, his gaze overly interested in the figures before him.

"Tired. And depressed."

His eyes shot to Dillon's. "You saw her?"

Dillon shook his head. "I'm persona non grata right now. Angie told me."

"Angie, is it? What's up with that?"

"Hey, you're the one who suggested I might take Angela out sometime." Dillon knew he hadn't said that, but it was worth getting a rise out of his friend just to shake him some.

"I did not. She's too young for you," Richard argued, consternation written on his features.

Dillon shifted, sitting up in his chair. "Oh, excuse me. You simply said Angela was a fount of information about Samantha and you wished you could get as lucky. Of course, you said it in my presence and with that forlorn puppy look."

Scowling, Richard replied, "I don't have a forlorn puppy look."

Dillon snorted.

Richard grunted and jerked the papers back in front of him. With a flourish, he began to sign.

"Careful. I might have slipped my resignation in there."

It might have been funny how fast Richard stopped his signing to look back through the papers, if only it weren't so obvious a sign of how distracted he was over Samantha.

Finally Richard lifted his gaze to his friend's. "Have I been that bad?"

Dillon sobered. "No, man. I'm so glad you're back right with God or I really might have had to put up with some problems. But at least there's one positive thing in your life right now—you're easier to deal with than if you were still frustrated over your relationship with God too."

"Thanks," Richard said.

Dillon wasn't sure if it was meant sarcastically or not. Still, he decided to return to the subject he'd been avoiding for three days now, the subject he'd decided to discuss with Richard before entering the office. "You haven't called her," Dillon said again.

"She didn't want me to," Richard replied.

"She didn't want you to for the past eight weeks." Dillon was determined to get through to Richard this time.

Richard simply made a face of displeasure at

being reminded of such a thing and then went back to signing.

"Why did you stop calling?" Dillon prompted, when Richard said nothing else.

"She's not taking my calls." Richard didn't look up, but continued to scan documents and sign them.

Dillon sometimes thought his friend was obtuse. "You know what your problem is, Richard?"

Richard sighed and put down his pen. "I suppose you're going to tell me."

Dillon nodded. "Yes, I am." He leaned forward, clasping his hands between his knees. "You're too used to snapping your fingers and having people jump."

Richard snorted. "Yeah. Right. If that were the case, this place would be open by now." Richard waved a hand around him. True, the office still wasn't completely furnished—though it looked better than the other offices—and the inside of the building was still pretty much a shell, waiting to be stocked, but that wasn't what Dillon meant.

Dillon shook his head. "I'm serious." Sitting back in the chair, he rested his arms on the soft leather. "You used to amaze me with your fiancée. When you two were at a party, all you had to do was nod your head and she came running. A slight twitch and she was making excuses why you two had to go.''

''She and I had a rapport,'' Richard said, defending himself.

''It's called power,'' Dillon countered. ''You do the same thing with the employees who surround you. A tilt of your head, a frown or a furrow of your brow sends them scurrying for whatever they feel it implies.''

Richard scowled.

Dillon smiled. ''It doesn't work with me, however. Nor, might I say, did it work with Samantha.''

Richard let out a long-suffering sigh. ''Your point?''

''You're so used to people jumping that you have no idea how to handle someone who doesn't, like Samantha.''

Richard started to argue.

''Hear me out. The first week you could understand her avoiding you, since her grandmother had just died. Besides, she'd just found out about you. She needed some time. Even for two or three weeks or even a month you could justify her being busy. But it's been eight weeks and she's still avoiding you. Instead of running to your side at your call, she finds an excuse to stay away. And that has you stumped.''

Richard sat for a moment, completely still, before his shoulders slumped. ''I don't know how to handle her.''

Now they were getting somewhere, Dillon thought.

Changing the subject, he said, ''Tell me again about that garden your grandda surprised your grandma with.''

Richard looked up curiously. ''What?''

Dillon raised a hand. ''Just humor me.''

Richard nodded. ''I was about six years old. I barely remember it. I do remember that grandma was wanting flowers. She loved flowers but had trouble getting around and digging beds. Grandda surprised Grandma with a huge garden out back of the house. He hired workers to put everything in, including already-blooming flowers. And the way he set it up was that it would bloom nearly year-round.

''Of course, she had a friend that was in on it. Grandda needed help and had her pretend she was sick. And Grandma went to take care of her little ones until she felt better. It was a ruse, however. Grandda says it was his way of showing his love to the woman who held his heart.''

''Sometimes actions speak louder than words,'' Dillon added.

Richard looked surprised by Dillon's statement. ''Yeah.''

''And that though he loved her, he'd never been able to give her something just for her, something that would touch her heart.''

Richard nodded. ''That's right.''

Dillon lifted both hands and shrugged.

Finally, the light went on in Richard's head. Swiveling his chair, he looked back out into the darkness toward the street, toward The Candy Shoppe. ''I just need to find a way to let her know I love her and make her feel special.''

Dillon was certain he'd exhausted his brain cells getting through to his friend. ''Think about it, Richard. Her dad left when she was a kid, then her mom left and was killed within the month. Her grandfather died. Then her grandmother had all of those strokes and ultimately left her with a business that is failing. She has never had one person be straight with her or make her feel like she was worth staying for. She's now losing her business, and you disappear.''

"It really does look like all I was after was information," Richard muttered.

"Yes. It does. You can call her and try to apologize all you want, but I don't think words are going to work on her. She's heard too many lies, Richard. She needs to see your feelings in action."

Richard swiveled back around. "I've been a fool. Wallowing in my own self-pity."

Dillon could hear anger in Richard's voice and was glad. He'd seen his friend moping around long enough. Never had he thought his friend was going to fall in love, but this woman, somehow, had captured his heart—and tied it into knots.

He was determined to see Richard end up happy.

If it killed him in the process.

"So, think, Richard," he said out loud. "What can you do that will inspire this woman to open her heart to you?"

For a long time Richard said nothing. He sat at his desk, staring off into space. Dillon watched Richard as the wheels turned. Though Richard appeared catatonic, Dillon knew that was simply how his friend looked when deep in thought.

And when he saw the slow smile curve Richard's lips, Dillon knew all was going to be well.

# *Chapter Thirteen*

"**W**hat are you doing here?"

Samantha glanced up at Angela's voice and saw Dillon entering her store. The tinkle of the bell sounded as well as a horn blaring outside as he entered.

"Angie." Samantha admonished her friend for her poor etiquette.

She finished putting the fresh candy up and then slipped off her gloves.

He looked as good as ever, Samantha thought, and she wondered if Richard looked as well. Dressed in a charcoal-gray suit, he strode up to the counter.

"And good morning to you as well, Angela." His gaze, however, was on Samantha.

"May I help you?" Samantha asked. She hoped he wasn't going to say anything about Richard. On the other hand, she wanted Dillon to mention him. Life was so unfair at times. Why couldn't she just get over him?

"I want two boxes of your best chocolates. The twenty-four-piece box."

"What are you doing, Dillon?" Angela asked.

Dillon's smile became strained. "I am trying to put in an order for chocolates, Angela."

"Angela." Samantha waved her hand.

Angela rolled her eyes and moved away to clean a table that some customers had just left.

Samantha noticed others who were there listening intently.

It figured. Everyone in town knew what had happened, so Richard's cohort showing up would only increase the interest of her regulars.

Samantha put on a smile. "Any preferences for those bests?" she asked, and pulled out a large box.

Dillon shrugged, an easygoing action he often used, and said, "Just your best."

Samantha didn't consider herself a mean person, but she knew Dillon had known all along just who Richard was...

She picked the most expensive pieces.

Dillon watched as she filled the box, not commenting. She finished filling it and then put the lid on it.

"How much do I owe you?" Dillon asked, pulling out his wallet.

Samantha named the price. Dillon grinned and handed her a credit card.

Guilt touched her as she swiped the card. Glancing back at Dillon, she said, "I have some cheaper pieces if you'd like."

Dillon chuckled. "Oh, no." He shook his head. "Don't worry at all. These are for Richard and, personally, I think he deserves to pay a high price for the candy."

At the sound of Richard's name, Samantha shook. But she didn't do the first thing she wanted to do, which was to ask how he was doing.

She didn't need to. Richard was buying chocolate. He'd given up on her and was back to his old ways.

Oh, she knew his ways, all right. She'd seen him on various TV shows. Now she realized it; before she hadn't. People just didn't look the same off-camera as they did on-camera. She would never forget that again. It wasn't unusual to see beautiful stars on his arm at certain functions. All of her customers had loved filling her in on just what they knew of him once they discovered who he was.

How had she thought she could attract a man like that? She probably seemed like such a small-town girl to him.

Determined to stop belittling herself, she pushed those thoughts aside.

She swiped the card again, waited for approval and then printed a receipt.

Dillon signed it, accepted the two large boxes and slipped them under his arms. "See ya," he said, grinning like a cat who'd just gotten a pitcher of milk.

He waltzed out.

"What was that all about?" Tessa Slater asked from the table where she and her husband, Drake Slater, had been having cinnamon rolls and coffee for breakfast.

Samantha lifted her shoulders in ignorance. "I suppose Richard has finally found another woman to stalk," she muttered, loud enough for the entire shop to hear.

Turning back to the counter, she went back to work and forced herself to put aside thoughts about Richard.

When a local deliveryman showed up not even an hour later, holding a large teddy bear with a box of her candy tied to its front, many of those customers who had heard Samantha's smart-aleck reply were still around.

They couldn't miss the announcement when, in a purposely loud voice, Chuck, the FedEx man, said, "Rush delivery for Samantha Hampton from Richard Reilly Moore."

Samantha's mouth fell open.

Her cheeks turned crimson.

"Wow! How cool. That bear is one of those popular ones that costs a fortune!" Angela said.

When Samantha didn't reach for the present, Angela did.

Chuck grinned at Samantha. He was one of her regulars.

"How could you help that man out? I'm sure he didn't go through regular channels to mail that," Samantha said, embarrassment getting the best of her.

"I'm on an early lunch break and he paid me well," replied Chuck.

Angela shoved the bear at her.

"He delivered my own candy to me!" Samantha said.

*Ooh*s and *aah*s sounded from all around her.

Okay, so it was original, Samantha thought. The bear was so very soft and huggable.

And she loved stuffed animals.

Richard couldn't know that, however. She smiled slightly, then realized what she was doing. "This doesn't make up for his lies," she announced.

Smiles left many faces.

She shoved the stuff back to Angela. "Please go put this in the living room. I have customers I need to serve."

"Come on, Samantha, admit it was something nice for him to do," Tessa called out.

Samantha shrugged. "It was a last-ditch effort on his part," she called back.

The noise level rose at the tables as everyone started talking about what had just happened.

Chuck ordered one of the prepackaged sandwiches and a cup of her espresso coffee and then took a seat at a table.

"I can't believe this," Samantha muttered when Angela returned.

"It's an apology," Angela said simply, and waited on the next customer.

"I don't want an apology," Samantha snapped at Angela. "I just want him to go back to New York and leave me alone."

"It ain't gonna happen," Angela replied, turning from the counter as the other customer left. "He's told you he loves you."

"But he lied to me."

"So did your family," Angela argued.

Samantha sighed.

Angela changed tacks. Cocking her head slightly, she studied Samantha. "Why won't you let Richard back into your heart?"

Samantha hadn't been asked that question in the past two months. She'd heard questions like, "Where is that young man you were dating?" or "What happened to your boarder?" or "Has he apologized?" And of course, comments like, "Oh well, it was never meant to be." "People can't fall in love at first sight." "He's a big man in business and wouldn't have stuck around such a small town." "Wow, he dates the rich and famous."

But to be asked outright why she wouldn't let him back in?

"He hasn't asked," Samantha finally said. "Besides, if he did, he's not sticking around here. And I have no desire to leave Hill Creek. And I'm not into the huge galas he attends."

"One," Angela began, "sometimes men don't know how to ask. Perhaps his calling to see how you are doing and dropping those hints that if you are hungry, he'd be glad to take you somewhere are his attempts to get back into your heart. Two, I can't see anyone wanting to simply stay in this town if they had a catch like that. And three, you love going to parties. You're just afraid you'd do something gauche."

"So?" Samantha replied defensively. "I'm a small-town girl used to small-town ways. But all of that is moot. He doesn't love me. He only said he loved me to find out information on the store. And now that he has what he wants, note that he hasn't come back around. This is simply a way to ease his guilt."

Angela rolled her eyes. "Well, we'll see about that. Won't we."

Her shop was nearly filled for breakfast the next morning as people milled around.

"Doesn't anyone around here work?" Samantha muttered, swiping hair out of her face as she brought out a fresh batch of rolls. "I've cooked so many of these, my double-chocolate brownies are still sitting back there waiting to be decorated."

Angela laughed. "Boy, are you in a bad mood. If you haven't realized, this is good for business."

"Hey, look at this!" Laura McCade said, walking into the store.

Others turned to see what the deputy sheriff was talking about. She held a newspaper in her hands.

"What is it?" Samantha asked, concerned.

Laura grinned. She turned the paper around and Samantha nearly dropped the pan of cinnamon rolls.

"'Dunnington's specializes in our own specialties,'" Angela read.

And directly underneath that was a picture of her candy shop and a full-page article.

"I'll kill them," Samantha said, her face heating up. She carefully set aside the cinnamon rolls and leaned forward to reach for the paper.

"What does it say?" one woman called out. Others echoed her question.

So, instead of handing Samantha the paper, Laura McCade began to read:

''Set to open, July Fourth, because of a delay caused by an electrical fire that prevented it from opening Valentine's Day, Dunnington's may be having second thoughts—or at least one member of the Dunnington family is. Richard Reilly Moore, often seen jet-setting to major cities where new Dunnington's Specialty Stores are opening, confessed that, while his own shops have worldwide items that can attract visitors, one special shop right here in Hill Creek is his main attraction.

''The Candy Shoppe, established by one of our own town's founding fathers, creates candies that Mr. Moore says are unique and definitely worth checking out. He suggests the praline fudge drops, saying the texture will leave your mouth watering for more.''

Laura laughed. Then she added. ''Listen to this. 'On another note, Richard and shop owner, Samantha Hampton, have recently been seen around town as a couple. Could it be that Richard Moore is now specializing in something other than specialties from around the world?' It then mentions the recent loss of your grandmother and how your store is still a great place for breakfast or lunch or a box of chocolates for that someone special.''

She finally held the paper out to Samantha, who snatched it and read the entire article. She ignored all of the excited murmuring as people questioned Laura about the story. When the morning papers were delivered to her shop fifteen minutes later, they sold out almost immediately.

"I'll order more," Angela said, and picked up the phone.

"No, wait—" Then Samantha simply gave up.

"Why would he do this?" she asked Laura, who stood there in her uniform drinking a cup of tea.

Laura smiled at her. "Isn't it obvious?"

Samantha shook her head. "I have no idea. I wouldn't advertise someone else's business in the paper, and that's basically what this boils down to—free advertising for my store."

"Along with an announcement about his feelings for you."

"What?" Samantha picked the paper back up, suddenly seeing it as Laura did.

"Anyone who would make sure your store got

that much advertising is definitely announcing that he cares for you.''

''But he doesn't say it,'' Samantha said weakly.

Laura laughed. ''That's a man for you. However, seeing who just pulled up in front of the shop, we might hear those words yet,'' she replied, turning her attention from Samantha to the man who was getting out of the car—with a guitar.

Oh! And there was Stephanie Collins, the reporter who had written the article. She had a cameraman with her, and they were following the guy who was dressed up as a minstrel into the store.

She didn't know who he was, but she did know they had a new business on the other end of town that delivered sing-o-grams.

''Samantha Hampton?'' he asked, after stepping into the store.

People on the street had noticed him.

The front windows were drawing a crowd.

The crisp, windy air blew in as someone held the door open so they could hear.

Samantha raised her hand to let the man know she was the person he sought.

She watched as he lifted his funny-looking round guitar and began to play.

And when he began to sing, Samantha's jaw dropped.

It was a familiar tune, but with Samantha's name placed in the lyrics. A love song, about unrequited love and how two lovers were separated....

"I can't believe this," Samantha said, not sure whether to cry or laugh. She winced as the photographer snapped her picture.

"Well, since most of the store is excited and more people are coming in, I think I'd be happy— though really embarrassed," Angela added, her face showing delight.

But when the minstrel ended with,

*"For I am still thy lover true
   Come once again and love me."*

Samantha simply stared, her heart pounding at those words. Nothing else would she remember but those last two lines. If only it had been Richard saying them, she thought as the sound of the music faded away.

There was a heartbeat of silence before the entire store erupted into applause. People crowded in, laughing and cheering the young man until he was quite red in the face.

He grinned and swaggered out of the store, finally accepting the praise.

"So, what are you going to do?" Angela asked.

"Hey, yeah," some young guy called out. "I'd like to know that. If it works, I might try it on my girlfriend."

The entire store burst into guffaws.

Samantha had never felt such pressure.

"Yeah, I'd like an answer, too," the reporter called out.

Camera flashes continued to go off.

"Richard has totally embarrassed himself for you. I think that should count for something," Mitch said.

Oh great, she thought. Mitch stood in the doorway. And more people were gathering because of the uniform, trying to see what was going on.

Mitch had evidently called his wife, because she was coming in right behind him. "Oh! I missed it," she cried.

"Not to worry. I have a copy on video," someone called out.

"What?" Samantha cried.

"I can't wait to send this to the TV station," that same person said, and went rushing out.

"He's created a snowball effect. Just wait," Stephanie said with enthusiasm.

Samantha groaned.

"So, what are you going to do? Come on. You can't just leave him hanging!"

Samantha thought and thought. She shook her head. "Come back tomorrow and I'll let you know," she finally said.

There were mutters of disappointment, but there was one thing for certain: she was going to have to bake twice as many cinnamon rolls for tomorrow.

# *Chapter Fourteen*

"**W**hat is this fax I got this morning from one of your employees?"

"Hello to you too, Dad," Richard murmured wryly to the speakerphone. Glancing over at Dillon, who had just entered his office, he lifted an eyebrow in query.

Dillon held up the fax he'd just sent not five minutes ago. Then, with a smile, he shrugged.

"Good morning," his dad said gruffly. "Now answer my question," he said, the speakerphone definitely allowing the agitation in his voice to be heard. "Did you really give this interview—and this business—to a local store owner?"

Richard leaned back in his chair. He had been

sitting in the office watching the crowd around The Candy Shoppe get larger and larger after the minstrel entered. Then he'd seen the minstrel leave, but the cameras and newspaper people were pushing their way through, still interested.

He'd been enjoying the show, wondering what Samantha was going to do, when his phone rang.

"Did I give the interview? Yes. I thought it might be good for business to give the local newspapers the personal touch and show a compassionate side for a local business."

"And giving that shop a load of business that should be ours, I'd bet," his father grumbled.

Dillon, who had walked over to the window, pointed to Samantha's shop and grinned.

"It might have," Richard replied.

"What were you thinking?" he demanded.

Richard smiled as he watched the people going in and out of Samantha's store. "Maybe I wasn't," Richard said. He could hear the sigh of frustration on the other end. "Listen, Dad, Samantha makes great candy. She deserves the business she gets."

The outrage in his voice was obvious. "She's our competitor, son. Wait a minute— Samantha.

You know her? You've been consorting with her? What's going on down there?''

Richard's smile faded. ''Not as much as I'd like, but I'm trying to remedy that. Listen, Dad, it's a long story. But, if I play my cards right, you may be getting a call this week announcing that I'm engaged.''

''Oh, son, please tell me it's not to the competitor.'' His dad sounded like he was going to cry.

Dillon chuckled, covering his mouth and turning so he wasn't picked up on the speakerphone.

''If I'm lucky. I gotta go. Someone is here. Talk to you later,'' he said, and hung up the phone despite his father's sputtering.

Richard turned to Dillon. ''You sent a fax to my dad?''

Dillon nodded. ''Five minutes ago. He's faster than I thought.''

''When it comes to business things, he can be pretty quick.''

Richard stood and stared out the window. Though it was a bright spring morning with the sun shining, no one could see him standing there. The windows allowed a person to see out, but not in. He noticed a few people drive by and look up—one was the reporter with whom he had spoken yesterday.

"When I told you to become proactive, I wasn't expecting this." Dillon's voice rang with delight.

"I'd love to be over there right now to hear what's being said," Richard said longingly.

Dillon chuckled. "I'm sure Angela will give me a report."

Richard turned slightly to study his friend. "So, what is up with you and Angela?"

Dillon waved a hand in dismissal. "She's a sweet kid, but too young. No, she and I have been pooling information. Angela is worried that Samantha is making a mistake by avoiding you. So, we've been chatting, you might say, to keep the lines open."

Richard frowned. "I should like to keep my business to myself."

Dillon hooted with amusement. "If that were so, you wouldn't have given that interview or sent that monkey over there to sing to your Samantha."

"She's not mine yet," Richard muttered.

"Sure she is," Dillon said, grinning. "She's

always been yours. She just hasn't realized it yet.''

Richard shook his head. ''Sorry, Dillon, but she has a choice.''

''Do you really think love has a choice?'' he asked mildly.

Richard started toward the door. ''In this case it does. I need to see how the campaign is going for our store opening. Are you going to be at the meeting?''

Richard knew he sounded short, but then, it was only because he was on pins and needles while waiting to find out Samantha's reaction.

Dillon didn't take Richard's tone to heart. He laughed. ''Don't worry,'' he said as if reading Richard's mind. ''We'll know by tonight or tomorrow how she reacted.''

''I hope so, because I only have one thing left, and if that doesn't work—''

He jerked open the door and nearly ran down his grandfather.

''Grandda!''

Even Dillon was surprised to see him. ''Mr. Dunnington,'' Dillon said respectfully.

Edward Dunnington Senior was in his eighties. Most of his hair gone and his face covered in wrinkles, he nonetheless had an aura of power about him. He stood there now, leaning on his cane, two executives behind him.

''I need to talk with my grandson,'' the old man said.

People scattered.

Dillon looked up to Richard.

Richard replied, ''Go tell the publicity people we'll have the meeting after lunch.''

Dillon nodded and left.

''Come in,'' Richard said, holding the door.

His grandfather shuffled slowly into the office. Dressed in a dark three-piece suit, he carefully made his way to a chair and lowered himself into it.

Richard leaned out to the secretary. ''No interruptions,'' he said, and closed the door.

Going over to the other chair, he sat down by his grandda. ''What are you doing here?''

Edward Dunnington tsked. ''Don't I get a hello?''

Richard's brusque attitude faded. ''Hello, Grandda. How are you?''

Edward's weathered face twisted into a caricature of a smile. ''Doing fine, I am. Missing Ireland. I'm already wantin' to go back. How about you?''

Richard shrugged. "Opening another store."

His grandfather placed both hands on his walking stick. "Is that so?"

He loved his grandfather dearly, but had no idea why the man was here. "You normally don't show up at the stores unless there's a special promotion, Grandda, so why don't you simply tell me what's going on. Then I'll know how to proceed."

His grandfather chuckled. "I can't fool you none, can I, boy? Well, as you know, this store is being made into a hub. I'm planning to see it run the entire southwestern region. I thought your young friend, Dillon, might make a good hub vice president."

Richard was pleased. "He'd like that."

"Then again, you might, as well."

Surprised, Richard only stared at his grandda. "Me? But—" He wasn't sure how to finish that.

His grandda, never at a loss for words, filled in the rest of the sentence. "You're set to inherit the business one day and therefore you have completely different duties. You don't have time to settle down and simply oversee a section of the country. Is that what you were going to say?''

Richard shrugged. ''My job has been pretty much set in stone.''

Edward nodded. He pushed himself up and shuffled over to the window, where he could look out. One of his white bushy eyebrows went up. ''What's going on down there?'' he asked, and pointed.

Uncomfortable, Richard cleared his throat. ''That's an, uh, it's a candy shop.''

The old man showed surprising agility as he turned. ''Oh, now? Is it?''

He could never keep a secret from his grandda. ''Yeah, it is.''

''The one I read about in the paper on the way from the airport?''

Richard nodded.

Edward tottered back over to a chair and eased himself down again. ''So, why don't you tell me, boy, what's going on here? 'Tis true I've known for a while you were disenchanted with life. I've watched you float along, simply existing, while it passed you by. When I heard about the fire and realized the store opening had been pushed off to near July, I started praying for an answer, I did.

That's when I decided to come visit. It's not often I get out and see my stores before they're actually open. I thought you might need a bit of encouragement or maybe a boost, since things have been going downhill for you lately.''

"Downhill?'' Richard asked.

His grandda shrugged. "You losing that fiancée I didn't like and then the argument you had with your da just before coming down here. You didn't think I knew about that, did you, boy? Your da told me. He loves you but isn't real good at showing it. So, when your da called me about the fire, I decided to come after things had calmed down a little.'' His grandda simply stared at him. "After reading the local paper, I'm glad I did.''

"You don't have to lecture me, Grandda, Dad already did.''

"Oh, did he, now?''

Richard nodded.

Edward chuckled. "I can only imagine what he had to say to you. Now, why don't you tell me about this woman who might be getting you to specialize in something other than candy.''

Richard flushed at hearing the quote from the paper. However, he respected his grandfather and would not hide what had happened from him.

"We met outside of church. That's how I ended up with a broken foot."

Edward's gaze narrowed. "I thought you were limping a bit."

"I've got the cast off, but it's still bothering me a bit. I'm sure the limp will be gone in a few more weeks."

"So, what did she do? Think you were a mugger and attack you?"

Richard chuckled. "No. Actually, Grandda, I was going into church and she'd forgotten her purse and was coming out. She ran into me and we both slipped on the ice and fell."

"I liked the mugger scene better," his grandda grouched.

"Sorry to disappoint you," Richard said wryly.

"Well, go on."

Richard shrugged. "I fell in love."

"When?"

"When what?" Richard tried to evade the question.

"Me. When I met my wife, it was love at first sight, it was. Very similar to your story, except that she was dirt poor and riding a horse into town to do some trading. She somehow managed to shove me into the back of the tiny cart, haul me back to her da's house and treat me there. I was unconscious for two days."

"I never knew that," Richard said. "You said she'd knocked you off your feet, but I thought…"

Edward chuckled. "She didn't like people to know. Anyway, I opened my eyes and knew from that moment on that she was the woman for me."

Richard nodded. "That's how I felt." He got up and strode across the room. Slipping his hands into his pants pockets, he stared out at the store two blocks away.

The breakfast crowd would soon be leaving Samantha's store and people wanting to buy gifts would be arriving. "She owns a candy store. I've tasted some of the things she makes and she is an excellent cook."

"So what's the problem?"

"She's not a good businesswoman. She doesn't know how to draw people into the store."

The creak of leather from the chair as his grandda stood sounded loudly in the room. In only a short time his grandda stood next to him. "So, you just helped her out by putting that article in the paper."

"I felt I owed her that."

"Why did you owe her, Richard?"

Richard sighed. "It's a long story, but basically, when I first met her I was so caught up in the feelings that I forgot to tell her that I was a Dunnington. She thought the chain was out to get her."

His grandda hooted. "She's got spunk, has she? And don't be lying to me. You didn't forget. You were scared to tell her."

"What was I going to say to her? Hey, I fell head over heels for you, Samantha, and that's why I didn't think about telling you who I was?"

"We're a very emotional lot, boy. It probably would have been best if you'd said just that. But then, they always say hindsight is twenty-twenty."

"It sure is," Richard replied.

"So, she got mad, did she?"

Richard nodded and proceeded to fill him in. "That brings me to my earlier proposal," said Edward, turning and shuffling back to sit down.

"About the vice president's job."

Edward nodded. "Your grandmother never liked traveling much and I didn't after I got married. Your dad was the same way until your mother died. And now he's getting too old to do much traveling."

Richard nodded. "That's why I'm doing it."

"That's true," his grandda admitted. "But I realized when that fiancée of yours left you, that you really have no time for your own life. This business has grown too fast. Therefore, I've been talking with your da. We're planning on a major restructuring.

"We are going to need five people to manage the business. Two will handle European and Latin acquisitions and development. They'll be based in New York and Dublin. Then we're planning to have three people overseeing the business in the United States."

"You're putting the company into other people's hands?" Richard was surprised.

"Not at all. Your uncle is going to handle the Dublin office. He already does a lot for me there since I can't really do much anymore. He's going to split stock with your father and your aunt. Your aunt loves New York and she's going to be there. Your cousin Sean will be running the eastern United States. He always was a momma's boy and wants to be near your aunt. And then I have the northwestern part of the U.S. I was going to offer you or Patrick. However, I think I've decided on Patrick to handle that."

His uncle's oldest son, Patrick, had attended school in Oregon and would probably enjoy that.

"You offered me the vice presidency."

Edward shrugged. "You can take the new vice president's position over the southwestern states and oversee this section, and keep Dillon on as your assistant. When I realized you'd found someone, Richard, my boy, I thought you might want to simply stay put and run the store. That's why I mentioned Dillon. However, I really want the stock to stay in family hands. So, if you take the job, you could keep Dillon as an assistant to go to the different stores as needed and do the traveling. It would give you time to settle down and raise a family."

Richard smiled.

Edward returned the smile.

"I'd have to see if Dillon is interested," Richard replied.

Edward nodded.

"And Samantha. She still isn't talking to me."

"I think you can settle that," Edward said.

"I was planning on it. Tomorrow morning."

Edward simply stared at him.

"I'll see what I can do."

Edward nodded again. "I'll be glad to help in anyway I can."

Richard thought about his plans and decided he needed to prepare and set things in motion.

Turning to his grandda he said, softly, "Thanks for showing up. How did you know I needed you?"

Edward simply smiled. "When God is in control and you're listening to his voice, things happen."

# Chapter Fifteen

*"Extra, extra. In today's Extra spotlight we have Richard Reilly Moore of that famous Dunnington's Specialty Stores."*

"Oh! Samantha!"

Samantha, who was finishing up the five o'clock rush, paused in what she was doing to turn toward Angela. "What is it?"

Angela pointed at the small TV behind the counter.

Samantha's eyes widened. "That's here! They interviewed Richard here. That's down by the mall!"

Others in the shop who had been drinking coffee and tea heard Samantha's shocked shout and immediately hurried over to the counter to see what was going on. Richard was giving a short interview to a nationwide gossip show.

When he was done talking about Dunnington's, he brought up his personal life. ''Stick around and you just might meet my future wife, if the woman I have fallen in love with agrees.''

The reporter turned back toward the screen and said, ''Stay tuned tomorrow, people, and we'll let you in on Mr. Moore's secret.''

Samantha's knees felt like jelly. She could feel every bit of color drain from her face.

She heard the door jingle and realized someone had rushed out of the shop to go spread what she'd just learned.

''What is he up to?'' Samantha turned to Angela. ''You've been keeping company with Dillon. What's going on?''

Angela lifted her hands helplessly, but her eyes sparkled with excitement. ''I don't know, but wow! Do you know that show goes everywhere. Everyone watches it! He's one powerful man to manage that! Did you hear what he said about marriage?''

Samantha nodded.

''He was talking about you,'' Stephen Hampton said. She and her father had started talking on a regular basis, much to her surprise, and though he didn't push it, she knew that her dad thought Richard really cared for her.

Slowly, Samantha shook her head. "He couldn't have been. Why would he talk to them about me?"

"Are you crazy?" one customer called out. "He loves you. He's trying to show you that."

"Yeah, lady. Any guy who would go on TV like that has to have it bad."

Chuckles from the few people in the shop sounded loud.

"Don't you get it, Samantha? He really loves you and is trying to apologize."

Angela's words went right into Samantha's heart. "He really does love me," she whispered.

She raised both hands to her cheeks and could feel the stupid grin spreading across her face.

"Well, duh!" a woman called out. "What was your first hint?"

Samantha's mind spun. The past few months whirled in her mind. Their meeting and then their unexplainable attraction that defied logic. "He really didn't mean to omit the truth, did he," Samantha whispered.

"Even if he did," Angela said, "don't you think he's paid enough for it? Sometimes we do stupid things that are wrong. He did something stupid. He's not perfect.''

''For two months, I wouldn't even talk to him.''

''I'd say he was discouraged, but something certainly changed his mind,'' Angela said cheekily.

Samantha turned toward Angela. ''You and Dillon?''

''I don't know. If it wasn't, it sure wasn't because we haven't been trying.''

''I love you,'' Samantha said, and pulled her into a huge hug.

''Uh-oh. He's at it again,'' a young male customer said to a friend. ''Making us look bad.''

''Hey man, now there's an idea. But I don't love any woman *that* much.''

''What?'' Samantha said, suddenly curious.

Heartbeat racing, she moved over to the edge of the counter and lifted it.

''Oh my,'' one woman said dreamily. ''If you don't want him, can I have him?''

People were gathering at the windows, peering out.

Samantha shoved between them, working her way to the door.

"Out of the way for my daughter," Samantha's father called out.

She made it to the door, but as soon as she jerked it open, she heard what they meant.

Bagpipes.

*Bagpipes on Main Street?*

She rushed out to the sidewalk and then simply stared.

The sheriff's men had shown up and were trying to direct traffic off the block. They'd cordoned off both ends of the street. Cameras were snapping along the sidewalks.

And coming down the street, dressed in a kilt, was Richard, a heart-shaped box clasped in his arms. Next to him was an older white-haired man, playing the bagpipes. And of course, Dillon was on the other side of the person, carrying a walking stick—for the old man, she presumed. Behind the three men was the minstrel who had visited the store.

And behind them was a huge crowd of townsfolk. There had to be two or three hundred, and the crowd grew even as she watched.

Samantha wiped her hands on her apron.

Angela quickly untied the dusty piece of cloth and pulled it off, then fluffed Samantha's hair.

"Stop that. Oh my!"

Her father gave her a gentle shove until she was in front of the crowd. "Go for it," he whispered, his voice filled with love.

The crowd continued to approach.

Samantha's stomach did flip-flops and sweat beaded on the back of her neck, not from the heat but from sheer nerves.

She looked at everyone and everything, except for the one person she wanted to see. She was afraid to find what was reflected in his eyes.

"There!" someone whispered, and pointed.

That was all it took. She was certain they were talking about Richard so she sought him out—and met his eyes.

She couldn't stop gazing at him.

He was gorgeous in that green plaid kilt. He wore a white shirt with a green, red and yellow plaid that crossed his chest and a purse that hung in front of him around his waist.

His kneesocks had tassels hanging off them.

Her mouth fell open. "He was the one who did those commercials so many years ago," she gasped. Though she hadn't recognized him, her mind was telling her that this was certainly the truth. Granny pulling on his leg, patting it. She'd been trying to tell her.

*Ooh*s and *aah*s and whispers began.

She ignored them. "Done," Angela said, referring to one of Granny's words whenever Richard had been in the room.

"Granny was trying to tell me he was a Dunnington, not *done*. That magazine she kept grabbing had that company picture of a kid in a kilt. That was him as a teenager. Why didn't I realize it?"

Angela chuckled. "She knew! Besides, you've always been trusting and accepted people at face value—except your dad."

That had changed, she realized, thinking of her dad right there by her.

She turned back around, her gaze again on Richard as the parade approached. He was smiling, a big broad smile, his eyes glowing with merriment.

When they stopped and the bagpipes ended, his gaze turned serious. Dillon handed the old man his walking stick and stepped back slightly, his eyes on Richard.

Richard gave a slight nod and then the minstrel began to play.

And to Samantha's astonishment, Richard began to sing a song that was very recognizable. "Greensleeves" to some, "What Child Is This" to others—the tune was the same. She didn't know a person who didn't know the song.

But then, when Richard started the second verse, he changed the words.

*"I have been ready at your hand, to grant whatever you would crave;"*

Did he mean that? Samantha smiled.

*"I have both wagered life and land, Your love and good will for to have."*

Well okay, he hadn't wagered land, she admitted, but he sure had his life when she'd run him down that first night they met. Samantha's heart broke open. Both hands went to her mouth and tears filled her eyes. But as he started the chorus, he changed it.

*"Sa-ma-an-tha-a, marry me! I'll live here with thee every day;*
*For I am still thy lover true, Allow me in-n and love me."*

The music died down.
The street was so quiet that the slightest noise

could be heard: a foot shuffling, a bag of groceries being shifted from hand to hand.

Richard wasn't done, however. After a heart-beat, he stepped forward from everyone and stood before her.

Dropping to bended knee, he held out a heart-shaped box of candies—the very ones she'd packed.

"Open them," he said softly.

The people around her held their breath.

"Richard, I—" she started, about to confess her love.

He shook his head.

Slowly, hands trembling, she pulled off the red ribbon. Lifting the lid, she looked in. The candy was all arranged the same, except for the very middle piece.

Where it had been, a tiny box now sat.

She steadied the candies on one hand and re-moved the box. Then Angela took the candy from her.

Samantha's eyes were glued to the box. Slowly, she flipped back the lid.

A collective *ooh* went up from the women around her.

Inside was an old-fashioned platinum ring with

a square-cut diamond surrounded by emeralds and rubies.

She lifted it out of the box.

"It was my grandma's ring," Richard said. "Grandda got it for her and passed it on to my mom when Grandma died. It's mine now, to give to the woman I ask to marry me. I've never given this to another woman to wear. It's a bit old-fashioned," he said.

Samantha's lips trembled. Lifting her fingers to them, she covered them.

Tears slipped down her cheeks.

"Do you want something contemporary?"

She shook her head. "It's gorgeous."

The old man piped in, "Told you that other fiancée wasn't worth her weight when she looked down on your mom's wedding ring. Glad you never had the chance to buy her one yourself."

The entire crowd laughed.

Richard actually turned red. He didn't reply but waited until the laughter died down.

Standing, he came forward and took Samantha's hand. Looking deep into her eyes, he said, "I was a fool not to let you know immediately who I was, an idiot to think it would matter one way or another how you felt about me and a complete imbecile to hesitate these past two months about making my apology clear.''

"I too, was a fool, Richard. I was hurt and angry and reacted stupidly.''

Richard grinned slightly. "If you will wear this, I'd love for you to be my wife, but first, I want to make you a business offer.''

He didn't release her hands but stared into her eyes. "My grandda is reorganizing the company. I'll be here, at this store, for the foreseeable future. Dillon has agreed to stay as well and help me run the western-region stores.''

Cameras moved closer at his announcement, and Samantha realized this was going to be on the news tonight and all day tomorrow. Big news, these Dunningtons.

"I'll be glad to stay here and help you in the store if you'd like. But, I'd also like you to consider opening up more stores.''

Low murmurs from the crowds showed their surprise. "I don't understand," Samantha said.

"Your homemade candy. I'd like you to consider bringing your company into the twenty-first century and offering some of them in a new section of our store dedicated to 'the old way,' where you can still find homemade candies, not candies that have been mass-produced.''

Overwhelmed, Samantha stared at him. "Do I have to answer you now?"

Slowly, Richard shook his head. "The only thing you have to answer right now is if you'll marry me and spend the rest of your life with me, until death do us part."

Fresh tears fell. "Until death do us part," she whispered.

"Samantha—" Richard started.

Samantha raised her fingers to his lips and covered them. She nodded. "I like the sound of that."

A second passed and then two, and then someone yelled, "What'd she say?"

Richard turned toward the crowd, his face exuberant. "Yes! She said yes!"

Turning back around he pulled her into his arms and kissed her.

The crowd went wild.

\*   \*   \*   \*   \*

Dear Reader,

This story was such a delight to write. Just before I started it, I was diagnosed with MS. I lost my agent and I was scheduled for surgery. All within three weeks of each other!

I thought, well, this story isn't due for three months yet, I should just set it aside. Instead, I started rereading the first three chapters, and I realized what a wonderful story I had here. One little omission, one little lie, can destroy a person, and yet, God is so willing to forgive. We should be able to forgive those who upset us in the same way.

Thrilled that I had a story where the hero actually messes up, but so does the heroine in the forgiveness department, I started writing. I couldn't put it down. It absolutely flowed from me. Only one other story has ever done that—*A Matter of Trust,* my first Love Inspired novel.

I realized how much the story and its theme meant. Forgiveness. Boy, is it hard sometimes, but it's so necessary. Poor Samantha must learn that even though she has been deserted again and again, she has a heavenly Father who will never desert her, and she can keep her eyes on Him as an example of forgiveness and love.

I hope you can, too, as you go through the trials on the horizon and learn how to let go and trust God by forgiving or simply communicating with the person who is lying to you.

I always love hearing from readers! Hope you enjoy the story!

Blessings!

Cheryl Wolverton